BETTER LEFT UNSAID

SABIN PRENTIS

This is a work of fiction. All names, characters, places, and incidents are the product of the author's imagination. With one exception, any resemblance to real events or persons, living or dead, is entirely coincidental.

Published by Fielding Books

© 2017 Sabin Prentis Duncan

ISBN - 13: 978-0-9984885-1-6

ISBN - 10: 0-9984885-1-8

Fielding Books

PO Box 7931

Richmond, VA 23223

www.sabinprentis.com

Dedicated to my parents, Fred & Joanne Duncan.
Thank you for the push out of nest so that I could spread my
wings and soar.
I love you!

"The course of true love never did run smooth."

William Shakespeare
A Midsummer Night's Dream

CHAPTER ONE

MONDAY, JANUARY 6, 2014

T anya began every morning nearly the same way. Whether it was an hour or a handful of minutes, more often than not, she rose before the sun.

Her pre-dawn routine typically included yoga, reading, or sketching. It was important not to over-plan the morning; but instead, let the activity come to her. It was her way of being in the moment. Yet, her dislike for planning those morning moments seemed countered by the certainty that she would witness the rising of the sun with a warm cup of green tea.

Sunrise watching and green tea were the staples of her morning.

From their apartment, Tanya could see nearly all Downtown Detroit and a swath of the Detroit River. She would lean her left shoulder on the far edge of the large window, clasp her tea cup with two hands, and allow her thoughts to wander. Some days, she was smitten by how the early sun rays gleamed off the Renaissance Center. Other days, she would watch an intersection and note the gradual build-up of traffic. Occasionally, during these serene mornings, she would be joined by Stokely, who would stealthily ease behind her. In his own way, he wanted to respect her solitude and indulge in her company.

They never verbalized an agreement; but over time, the accepted manner of Stokely's arrival consisted of one deep inhale and slow exhale to announce his presence. Then a very slow, feathery caress that began with the tips of his middle fingers on the apex of her hips. From there in a span of ten to twenty-seconds, beginning with the rest of his fingers joined tightly together like a swimmer's cupped hands during their stroke, Stokely's fingers and then his palms would reach through the band of Tanya's pajama bottoms, gliding smoothly over her hips and pelvis while reaching toward the velvety softness of her upper inner thighs. Once there, he would gradually spread his fingers like an Oriental fan and then move his hands outward until the width of his finger span covered her thighs where the pockets of a pair of jeans would lay.

As he would begin to press his body against hers, the left side of his face would pass over her dreadlocks. Once at their end, Stokely would use the tip of his nose in a faint sweeping manner to move her dreads aside. With a bundle of her dreads along the side of his face, he would continue to use his nose to line the rim of her ear. His breathing would sometimes be slow, sometimes heavy, but always preceding the soft kiss he planted behind her earlobe.

Following his kiss, Tanya would lean back into his embrace. During these moments, their bodies said a more loving "Good morning" than their tongues could ever tell.

However, this morning none of that happened.

STOKELY'S ARRIVAL last night to a nearly empty apartment

didn't impart the message. Neither did the calls to Tanya's recently discontinued phone number convince him fully. Although his night was filled with worried sleep and empty reaches for Tanya, Stokely remained in steadfast denial.

The unpleasant truth dawned upon him incrementally just as the rays from the rising sun eked their way through gloomy clouds and into the living room window. The absence of Tanya's silhouette near the window caused Stokely to swallow hard as sad realization and begrudging acceptance cemented in his heart. He knew that Tanya would never start another morning leaning against this window. After assuming her former post at the window's edge and peering-out over the overcast Detroit skyline, he was now certain that she was gone.

The view revealed clouds so gray that they darkened the morning sky as if it were minutes before sunset. The gloom also reflected the melancholy pervading his heart.

She was gone for good. Leaving him a broken man with broken dreams to suffer in what some would call a broken city.

It is not easy being an architect in a place becoming more renowned for its decaying structures than new construction. What he once considered a side hustle, working as an adjunct professor for the local university's School of Architecture, had to his dismay become his sole source of income. He had drunk the Kool-Aid of urban revitalization thinking he could be a force against the rising tide of misfortune engulfing his hometown. But now his dreams of saving Detroit were secondary because he couldn't even save his love relationship and even worse, his home.

A generous signing bonus helped lure him back home from a more prominent firm in the nation's capital. Once back, he dove right into the American dream of home ownership, furniture be damned. Seriously, how many unmarried, childless, 27-year-olds need a four-bedroom house? But he could afford it.

Plus, home ownership was supposed to be a certain prosperous investment.

Eight years later, Stokely is still attempting to emerge from the bankruptcy swamp under which that house had nearly taken him. Like thousands of others, he had to walk away from his house and vacate his dreams. Like the others who made comparable choices, the consequences left his confidence rattled and his optimism calloused.

Previously, when professional opportunities arose that would have taken him to other cities, he declined. More accurately, he failed to heed the writing on the wall. Wall-writing like that is easy to ignore when one is engulfed in a love like theirs. Was it her love or maybe their sex that kept him? He wasn't sure nor could he untangle the mourning of Tanya's departure from the state of his hometown. Should he leave this place where it seems many have already left? The jobs are scarce and hope is declining. Plus, without Tanya, what's the point of staying?

The growling of his stomach reminded him that he could not stare out the window all day. But what else is there to do? His pride erected a damn to hold back the tears. His ego scrolled through memories of all the women he had encountered and could not recall another woman who could assuage this emptiness. His feet led him away from the window and into the kitchen.

Couscous - the sight of the small box of one of Tanya's culinary staples caused him to reflect upon a happier time when they were grocery shopping at Whole Foods. A day when he smirked with a pinched nose and a quizzical look as he teasingly asked, "What is this shit?" She gave him some type of organic-preserve-our-bodies explanation that he heard but did not listen. He chuckled as he remembered that he must be one of the few men ever who loved to hear their woman talk. Her voice had what could be described as a feminine huskiness to it - huskiness with a little scratch on it. To him, it was like she spoke with a heaviness that most women only have in an advanced state of arousal; which indirectly, aroused him.

He feigned ignorance so that she could talk. He listened, not often to her words, but always to her melodic timbre.

"Don't you see your body as a temple?" she asked after sharing her soliloquy on the health benefits of couscous. He mocked, "I have to eat conscious to preserve my temple?"

"Couscous, Stokely! Couscous."

"What are we eating Tanya? First, hummus and now, conscious."

"Stokely, you can say 'Couscous.'"

He grinned a playful and sardonic smirk before uttering, "Consciousness." She played along, punching him in the shoulder after placing a box of couscous into their cart. As she crossed the item off their list, he asked, "You know what you vegan-types are known for?"

She smirked with her hand on her hip. "What are we known for?" She asked sarcastically.

"You don't know?"

"If you don't tell me I'm going go Mayweather on you!" She replied while shaking her fist at him.

"I thought you knew."

"What Stokely?!"

He suppressed a smile before answering, "Your room-clearing farts."

She chased him down the aisle screaming, "I DON'T FART!"

The elderly man stocking items burst into laughter. Cornering Stokely between the display case of all natural tortilla chips and salsa made from locally grown tomatoes, Tanya delivered a combination of playful punches to his shoulder. She then commenced into a girlish pout as he wrapped his arms around her.

"I know honey. You don't fart, you poot." She tugged away from him as he joined the stock guy in laughter.

THAT WAS THEN, during happier times. Now, all that's left of hers is this couscous. "Funny," he thought, "how you can keep the memories longer than you can keep the woman."

He reached for the box, stared at it, and shook it intermittently. Then tossed it toward the trash. The box clipped the edge of the can before spilling onto the floor.

"Damn, can't even throw that shit away," he thought. While kneeling to the floor his thoughts returned to Tanya. Using the edge of his hand to gather the spilled items into a pile, he wondered if she was really gone this time.

How many times had she said, "I can't do this anymore!"? Too many.

How many times had she cried while they were making love? Only to answer her tears with the question, "Why can't we be forever?"

How many times would she manufacture an argument just for the hell of it? He would learn rather quickly that she essentially was venting and using him as a sounding board.

After scooping the last pile of couscous, he could gather with his hands into the trash, he leaned back onto the cabinets, wrapped his arms around his knees, and brought his head to rest on his forearm.

TANYA IS AN ENGINEER. A design engineer, she would

add, as if other engineers were not as smart or in some other way not as distinguished as design engineers are. They met last year at the African American Engineering Alliance (AAEA) conference hosted by his employer. As an adjunct architect professor, he was not invited to the event but when she passed him pulling a cart and walking with that just-a-shade-humbler-than-a-diva aura about her, he was magnetized. Thankfully, his ID badge was like the ones worn by the conference participants and he was admitted into her workshop without a hassle.

Even under Abu Ghraib torture, he would be unable to recall the topic of her presentation, as he was transfixed by her presence and beauty. He was sure she noticed his staring because during the Q & A time, she walked the aisle, fielded a question from the rear, and rested her hand on his shoulder. The way an elementary school teacher would do the kid who was fidgeting with things in his desk and the teacher would use subtle touch to redirect the kid to the lesson.

Except Stokely didn't need redirection, he was beyond focused. He was enthralled. Her hand on his shoulder only intensified his point of convergence. Afterwards, as the line of engineers sharing their appreciation for her research thinned, he lingered around studying the charts and graphs she had referenced during her session.

"So, you followed me?" She asked approaching him from behind.

He turned into her gaze. "The trifecta!", he thought. 'Trifecta' being an ode to one of the relationship conversations between men that women would never understand. That conversation placed a trifecta, a matching shade of brown skin, brown eyes, and brown hair, as an occurrence of luck on par with finding a four-leafed clover.

"The best choice I made all day," he responded.

She stopped. "Do you usually make bad choices?" She asked with a flirtatious hesitation.

He sighed, "Sometimes when things are too good to be true, I allow doubt to convince me otherwise."

She squinted as though peering through a fog.

"Did I say something wrong?" She stared a few seconds longer.

"You're transparent," she said softly.

Without realizing it, he stretched out his arms and looked down into his chest. Was he ghost? Was Bill Cosby going reach through him as Ghost Dad? "Transparent? Man, what the hell?" He thought.

She laughed. "No silly, you're not a ghost; you're honest."

He attempted to gather himself. He wanted to lie and say he wasn't thinking that she meant he was a ghost. But he didn't. He just blushed.

"I told you that you were honest."

He was puzzled.

"You were going to lie and say that you weren't thinking about ghosts. But you chose not too because you're honest."

He was in love already.

It was always unsettling how well she knew him. That feeling of how well she knew him further exacerbated the hurt of her sudden departure. Was it really sudden? Or had he missed the signs?

She had been upfront about her marriage. Her husband's career had prompted his relocation to Nashville. She chose to keep her job with Chrysler and thus the explanation for the living arrangement. Stokely was unsure if her husband knew she lived with another man during the work week. He was sure that if her husband found out, he would be, at the very least, angry.

"HOW THE HELL did she get all her stuff outta here in one day?"

He gathered himself from the kitchen floor and made his way back to the second bedroom that served as an office. His books were stacked against one wall and the futon where he slept was near the other.

He shook his head while wondering if his body would forgive him for opting for the cheaper, thinner futon mattress. Tanya had warned that the difference of $100 was not savings enough for such a flimsy mattress.

Damn, did she always have to be right?

CHAPTER TWO

TUESDAY

It was unusually warm for January. Warm being a relative term as the weatherman was reporting 42 degrees before Stokely tapped the power switch and tossed the remote to the futon.

The walk from the apartment to campus was not quite 3 miles. He knew that by the time he wrapped up his office hours, those 42 degrees would have worked their way down to 20 something. His mother would be proud that he dressed in layers and remembered a hat, scarf, and gloves. She would be much prouder of that than knowing her son had been living with a married woman.

That's why she didn't know.

As he made his way down the stairs, he thought of his father, with whom he confided Tanya's marital status. His dad tilted his head to one side, arched an eyebrow, and said, "Married, hunh?"

Then paused and added, "Son, be careful."

During another pause, Cleve, noticed his son was both love-struck and conflicted. To which he responded with a Chris Rock quote, "Look, I ain't sayin' its right; but I understand."

Understanding Stokely's love relationship was one thing, but making sense of how Stokely went from being an employed architect with his own home to an unemployed architect who had to walk away from his custom renovated home required an entirely different type of understanding. "Hell," Stokely thought, "I could walk from here to Chicago and still not have enough time to figure that out."

Stokely took the long way, crossing over the interstate and walking past the casino, boutiques, and eateries. While walking, he wished that his phone would vibrate from one of Tanya's cheerful mid-morning text messages. But he knew that wish was more futile than wishing Jesse Jackson was at a loss for words.

"Why are we doing this teenage shit? Can't we call each other like adults?" he recalled asking Tanya. "Stokely, stop being old fashioned. Maybe I just want to let you know I thought about you without striking up a conversation," Tanya replied.

He shook his head. Not that texting was a big deal. No, he just believed texting was trivial shit people did because they are more comfortable interacting with a damn device than with humans. Deep down, he knew his was just being contrary for no reason; but if texting made Tanya happy, then he would live with it.

The thought rehashed some of Tanya's other proclivities, like her demands that they only make love in the bedroom, because she likes to snuggle afterwards before going to sleep. Or that they must say grace before eating anything, even a cookie. Damn if either one of the has been inside a church in the last two years, she wanted to honor God for the blessing of nourishment.

There was also the persistent grammar check. No matter

the nature of conversation, she was vigilant about correcting his grammar. An exchange would go like this:

Stokely: Hell nawl, I ain't going to no damn back rack yoga class!

Tanya: It is bikram yoga and 'no, I would not like to participate.'

Stokely: Tanya, my mama's name is Elaine.

Tanya: Ok, Mister, your mother's name is Elaine. What does that mean?

Stokely: It means your name is Tanya. My ma's name is Elaine. Soooooo, you ain't my damn mama!

Tanya: You are not my mother.

He crossed a street near the stadiums. Both the football and baseball stadiums reminded him of the type of architectural work he longed to do. At one point, this juncture was abandoned buildings and warehouses, now it consists of architectural marvels that enhance the community. On the real, they probably didn't bring the projected thousands of jobs and millions in revenue for the city as had been promised; but that fight was for another soldier. Stokely only wanted to create new structures that integrated history while utilizing current innovations, sort of like blending the best of the old with the promise of the new. Isn't there a market need for someone like that?

"Like these dudes," thought Stokely as he crossed Woodward Avenue (in the middle of the street of course because crossing at the crosswalk in the city says things about a person). "These dudes" are reclining in a 1994 Chevrolet Impala SS. Given the lighting, the car would appear dark green, purple, or black. An old car sitting on (equipped with) dazzling chrome rims and tires shined to brilliance that captured Stokely's reflection. An old car enhanced with the latest gizmos loved by urban auto enthusiasts.

In a timeless, yet minimalist ode of respect, Stokely, with a steely jawed expression - a shade below neutral but in the direction of aggression - gives a three quarter of an inch head nod upward while looking the driver squarely in the eye.

The driver whose left shoulder is not visible from the outside but his right shoulder is perched high, perhaps in the center of the seat, and whose right wrist rests at 12 o'clock on the steering wheel returns the nod. The passenger was occupied with thoughts that facilitated his distant gaze out the other window. Had Stokely not been approaching the car while crossing the street, he would have figured the driver as the sole occupant of the car as the passenger was slouched so low. The Impala proceeded southward toward downtown to a heavy bass undergirded soundtrack and with 'Pac spittin' a verse from *Picture Me Rollin'*.

One thing for certain, unemployed architects masquerading as adjunct professors aren't rolling very far; hence Stokely's walk to work. Even more ironic, Stokely couldn't picture himself rolling and if he didn't do something about his revenue stream, rolling anywhere was going to be real complicated.

After arriving in the office he shared with another adjunct, he wasn't fully seated before there was a knock at the door.

"Excuse me, Professor Robeson? Do you have a moment?"

Stokely looked to the door. The Dean of the School of Architecture was peering in from the hallway.

"Uh sure, c'mon in." Stokely replied while thinking "I know he's not about to remind me of those boring faculty meetings that I don't have to go to."

Dean Griffin entered and gestured to the chair that belonged to the other adjunct professor. A retired architect, Stokely's fellow adjunct once shared, "Notice our little closet is near the trash chute? That's because we're the next thing to go!" He would follow the statement with cackled laugh that led into brief coughing spell. One could always tell when that adjunct was finished talking because he would repeat the last statement, follow it with a "Yes, sir," and then repeat it again. If he liked you, he'd mix in your name for good measure.

"The next thing to go Robeson, yes sir, we're the next thing to go."

"Professor Robeson, I wanted to share some good and bad news with you before you were ill-informed by the rumor mill," Dean Griffin stated conspiratorially. "It's no secret our enrollment has been declining for the last few years."

"Oh shit," thought Stokely repeating his officemate's suggestion, "The next thing to go. Yessir, the next thing to go."

Dean Griffin continued in half-conversation, half-verbalization of his fear-ridden opinion, "Our president believes we can inflate our numbers with a more robust online presence. As if you can teach architecture over the goddamn internet."

"To that means, the courses taught by adjunct faculty will be eliminated and replaced by the online courses taught by tenured staff. Robeson, this affects you because Dr. Coleman is on sabbatical - an indefinite one if you ask me - and we're going to need someone to cover his load both on the internet and the studio."

"So, I'm being let go?"

"Not quite Robeson," Dean Griffin paused to check his watch before continuing. "You're a throwback to how architecture should be. Your professors down at South Carolina A&M, they ..."

Stokely corrected his supervisor, "North Carolina A&T."

"Like the telephone company? Anyway, you were taught pure architecture. Some of these other whippersnappers your age rely on technology too much. They let the goddam computer do the designing. Pure architecture is visionary. It's from the heart. Not some goddamn software package."

Stokely could see this matter went deeper than the dean's

comments. But he was wondering if he was going to still have a job.

"Well that's the bad news; you'll be coming off the bench for Coleman and teaching Basic Drawing via the internet. You're going to need a sky pie account."

"Skype?"

"What?!"

"A Skype account - Skype allows you to talk to people face-to -face like via the internet."

"Is that what sky pieing is? How in the hell are you face to face over the goddamn internet? And you wonder why these whippersnappers can't design in real life!"

Stokely agreed but his agreement was choked with the uncertainty about whatever the 'good news' was.

Borrowing the Dean's terminology, Stokely asked, "Is coming off the bench for Dr. Coleman the good news?"

"I guess it could be. The Metropolitan Revitalization Organization is seeking to transform the old abandoned train tracks out of downtown into some type of communal fitness walkway. They are asking for a youthful, fitness-type architect with an appreciation of the city's history to act as a lead consult. Are you interested?"

Stokely wanted to shout, "Hell yeah!" But instead he inquired, "This is a paid consultancy, right?"

Dean Griffin replied, "Sure, but you probably would want to pay them in exchange for not having to attend those conservative, snobbish meetings. You know, given your disdain for boring meetings."

They shared a laugh; the Dean's was sarcastic compared to Stokely's nervous chuckle. Then Dean Griffin rose to depart.

Before proceeding down the hall, he leaned back into the office door, "There's a student out here and when you finish with her, make your way to the faculty meeting. Your colleagues may want to congratulate you!" With that, Dean Griffin lumbered down the hall laughing.

Stokely found himself doing a childish face while mouthing "Your colleagues may want to congratulate you," when she entered.

Her perfume reached his nose before her beauty caught his eyes. Not that the perfume was too heavy. It was far from heavy. It was a soft, pleasant fragrance that contrasted with the dusty odor of the old building. Almost like her scent wafted into his nostrils and anchored there.

She stood just over five feet with those boots, but he was sure she flirted more with 4′10″ than 5′1″.

"Professor Robeson?"

"Yes," replied Stokely.

He had never seen her before but secretly hoped that he would see her again, soon.

"All of the other offices were dark when I saw the light on in here and hoped someone could help me with some information."

She was all business, no flirting. Yet, her girlish features and professional posture were both alluring and disarming.

"Sure, have a seat. How can I help you?"

Her hands put her in her mid-twenties, but if one relied on a headshot with no make-up, she'd pass for seventeen, nine out of ten times.

"I'm with a small publishing company and we're doing a series of books on the city's ruins or decaying structures. I was hoping that an architect could provide a perspective on our photos and essays." She paused and then resumed, "I admit randomly visiting the School of Architecture is a shot in the dark, but I'd figure it was at least worth a try," she explained.

"Her lips, wow." Stokely thought. They made a small circle on her face. Her upper lip contained a sharp v or crease in the center that pointed downward to a bottom lip that was full and pouty. That pouty lip was enticing-bait that snagged attention for the unveiling of her smile. With her smile, she'd easily be both the Crest and Colgate Model of the Year. When her lips drew back to reveal the splendor of her smile, it was more heart-warming than a grandmother's embrace.

"I didn't get your name," he said while extending his hand for a shake.

"Oh, I'm sorry. I'm Phoenix Ellison."

"You're not from around here, hunh?" Stokely inquired.

"What do you mean by that?" Phoenix responded.

"Well, people around here, they are used to these buildings. It's the out-of-town folk who marvel at the decay. Plus, your accent doesn't fit the local drawl."

"I'm glad I don't have a drawl," she laughed.

"I'm from California, Vallejo to be exact. It's a small city in the Bay Area. We moved here when I started middle school. After high school, I attended Bennett College and then University of North Carolina at Chapel Hill for graduate school."

"You went to Bennett?"

Before she could respond, he blurted, "I'm an Aggie!!"

She smiled a relaxed smile that was more warming than her professional one.

He was going to ask when she graduated but thought that would be too much like asking her age. Plus, she mentioned grad school. He was pretty sure she had graduated, although there aren't many UNC grads in Detroit.

"What brought you back?" he asked in an effort toward conversation.

"It's a long story and I think you have a meeting to attend. Let's just say between this place and Vallejo, it's a tad perplexing that the places I consider home, their best days long preceded my best memories. This means some of the memories

I cherish and many of the foundational components of my identity are built upon decay."

It was obvious that she wasn't putting him on about it being 'long story.' He was self-conscious enough to maintain listening body language. So, when she stopped talking so abruptly it was startling.

There was an uncomfortable silence. To him, it seemed as if for a minute, she had opened the shutters of her soul and allowed the sun to shine-in only to see an unfamiliar face in her view prompting her to quickly close the shutters. Well, that analogy does not totally fit because to him, she is the sun shining out.

"Can we continue this talk later? Your perspective sounds interesting; yet, I need to get to this meeting. Count me in on your publishing project. Do you communicate via email or phone?"

She handed him her card and lingered a bit after standing as if she were walking out with him. He took the cue and while locking the door, he said, "I'm not sure how I can help but you can use me how you see fit."

When he turned, she was there. Not too close, but not exactly across the hallway either. For a fraction of a second, the shutters of her soul opened and that light shone through her eyes. This time, she gradually closed the shutters as if before waving goodbye. As if a cloud was passing, her warmth transformed into polite professionalism.

"Great, let's be in touch. We've already began shooting footage on the boulevard" were the words that came from her mouth. But Stokely couldn't help but think about the message she said with her eyes.

CHAPTER THREE

TUESDAY EVENING

With her arms folded, she shook her head and mouthed the words, "Only you."

Stokely looked surprised, raised his arms in surrender, and laughed when replying, "What?"

"Only you would have a playlist that goes from The Roots to The Culture Club to Walter Hawkins to Johnnie Taylor in consecutive songs," Tanya stated.

Stokely resumed singing along with Johnnie Taylor while washing dishes. Earnestly, Stokely was singing Taylor's *We're Getting Careless with Our Love* from the childhood nostalgia of overhearing his father play records after everyone was supposed to be asleep. He even had choreography in which he'd spin around in front of the sink and scream, "Wake Up!" on cue with Johnnie. However now, recalling that memory of singing that song in the presence of Tanya was accompanied by a piercing irony.

It was one thing to sing about carelessness in the company

of the woman he loved, but it was something entirely different to ponder if that carelessness cost him the woman he loved.

Tanya was gone and presumably with a new phone number, since his calls were answered with the "The number you have called is not a working number" message. After another futile attempt, he placed his phone on the counter and walked out of the kitchen. That was when he noticed an envelope near the door.

He took a deep breath. He knew that when something troubled Tanya she wrote long, often rambling letters. Picking up the envelope, it seemed to be a single page note. Only Tanya's "I love you" sticky notes could be as concise as whatever was in the envelope. Yet, those little notes were so random, Stokely ruled it out as a possibility for the enclosed message.

The envelope spelled out his full name STOKELY MEDGAR ROBESON. When he opened it, he saw that there was no letterhead and that it had been printed on linen paper. It read:

MR. ROBESON,

Allow me to introduce myself - I am Oscar Rousseau, III. I doubt that you know me, but I am Tanya's husband.

Your life with my wife is over. I am sure you can understand that. You can either accept it or else.

"Or else what, motherfucker?!" Stokely snarled as he balled-up the note. His anger was stoked by the vibrating sound of his phone against the countertop. He snatched the phone and read a text from an unfamiliar number.

UNKNOWN: Stokely, this is Tanya texting from a co-worker's phone. Don't text me back. Just meet me at Slow's in an hour. Please :-)

"DAMMIT!!!" He snapped aloud. His thoughts were, "What the fuck? This punk-ass Oscar then this stupid ass text. Man, what the hell is going on?"

His anger did not replace his longing for Tanya. Nor did it cloud his city instincts. He put on his shoulder holster and placed his dark blue 9mm Ruger in the left holster. He planned to walk to the grand casino and then take a cab to Slow's.

He loved Slow's. The crowd is eclectic and the bar bq is awesome. Good bar bq and a Guinness Stout makes for good times. Plus, he knew his plans of eating Frosted Mini-Wheats cereal for dinner was a poor excuse to skip Slow's.

WHEN HE ARRIVED, he grabbed the bar stool closest to the door so that he could scan the crowd. For some reason, he thought if he gave himself a few moments to gather his cool then his talk with Tanya would be more productive. He smirked slightly at his little ploy toward gaining some type of control of a situation that had grown out of his control.

"Whatcha drankin'?" the bartender interrupted.

Slightly annoyed, Stokely replied, "Guinness."

As the bartender turned, Stokely looked at the large hoops in the bartender's earlobes. The hoops and the fire flame tattoos on his neck led Stokely to assume that the bartender probably plays in a garage band and could skateboard his ass off.

"Hmph, stereotypes ain't shit. I'm a Black man with a terrible jump shot," he thought.

As Stokely reached for the glass, he noticed a party of three across the bar. A truly odd mix consisting of a Rick Rubin look alike, either a Hispanic or Arabic dude with crazy hair gel, and Phoenix.

She waved.

Stokely caught his drink before it spilt over the bar. The bartender had his towel ready and gave Stokely a head nod down. White and square black dudes nod down; brothers nod up.

Phoenix suppressed a laugh as Stokely waved back. Faux Ricky Martin looked in Stokely's direction. But Stokely didn't mind because his attention focused beyond Phoenix. In the booth past the bar, sat Tanya.

She was consumed with her phone and hadn't noticed him at the bar.

Phoenix beckoned for him to come. Stokely grabbed his beer and headed over.

"Professor Robeson, I'd like you to meet Pedro and Jake," said Phoenix as she gestured to wannabe Enrique Iglesias and ZZ Top. Stokely gives them a head nod. He wants to hug Phoenix, but instead whispers in her ear, "I have a personal matter to attend to now, but let's be in touch soon." She placed her hand on his arm and mouthed, "Okay."

Tanya watched.

"It hasn't even been a week," she complained.

"You left me," he snapped as his anger began to rise.

"Everything isn't about you Stokely. I ..." he cut her off. "You what?"

Tanya looked at her phone and bit her lip. The tapping sound could only be her tapping her foot under the table. Through pursed lips, she asked sarcastically, "Who is your little plaything?"

"That's none of your damn business!" he said louder and more defensively than he intended. Phoenix and Pedro turned from the bar.

Pedro said some shit to Phoenix that affirmed to Stokely that he would eventually have to kick Pedro's ass. But if it jumped off tonight though, he might shoot him. He doesn't want to shoot him because it would probably mess up his chances with Phoenix.

Stokely's heart skipped a few beats when he saw Phoenix. To him, seeing her with Tanya in the background made him imagine Phoenix in full view through the front windshield of his life and Tanya fading in the rear-view mirror. Except some mirrors warn that objects may be closer than they appear and right now Tanya was too damn close.

Jake said something that caused the two to turn back towards the bar. While Phoenix turned, Stokely took his time to take in the view from behind. The way she sat perched on the stool could be catalytic for the imagination.

"You're staring," Tanya chimed dismissively.

Annoyed, Stokely turned to face the woman who held his heart. He looked into the eyes of the one he trusted. The one who broke the heart he entrusted her to cherish. His anger began to rekindle.

"Your bitch ass husband slid a note under my door. What kind of hoe-assed shit is that?"

Tanya's face was ashen.

During the silence, Stokely stole another glance over at Phoenix. She seemed friendly and Pedro was working intensely to escape the 'friend zone.' Stokely looked over to Jake and imagined him as the type who could assess various qualities and quantities of cannabis. Phoenix was a sight to behold even if she was trying to dress down. She...

"So, you've moved on already?" Tanya asked.

"Hunh?" Stokely replied. He heard her but needed to buy some time to gather a response.

"The little girl at the bar, the one who can't probably buy a drink - are you interested in her?" The sarcasm in Tanya's voice overflowed like a clogged toilet. It also carried an overflowed toilet's repulsiveness.

With that, Stokely intentionally allowed his eyes to linger on Phoenix twice as long to irk Tanya further.

When he finally turned to look into Tanya's eyes, his eyes were an inferno of bitterness and his disposition was indifferently cold. Tanya's edge retreated and fear fluttered through her heart. Though clenched teeth, he stated with an intense frigidity, "It isn't like I don't have more than enough empty space to accommodate her."

His piercing glazed was unflinching.

Now Tanya was certain that their relationship was over. She also knew that no one could harbor feelings that intense unless love had been there. This is the other side of the coin. She found solace in recognizing that Stokely had loved her in a way she had not previously noticed. She accepted the beauty of what they had but her ego could not accept that he could move on so quickly.

"It was the abortion," she whispered.

The inferno in Stokely's eyes intensified.

"What...," he took a deep breath to control his temper and with pregnant gaps in his questioning - the type of gaps some of the old-school mothers would utilize when contemplating murdering their children.

"... are ...

... you ...

... talking...

about?"

As if the heavens opened, he heard in a distance, "Pedro, I'll take a cab. If you give me a ride home that may make you misunderstand our partnership."

"MUTOMBO-ED!" Stokely cheered silently as Phoenix swatted down Pedro's advances.

Engulfed in her own grief, Tanya missed the soft rain that tempered Stokely's rage.

"Normally, I handle all of the insurance information in our home. My OB / GYN referred me to a specific doctor for the procedure. Our insurance company called the house to inquire about our change in primary physicians," Tanya explained.

As if a somewhat transparent curtain had dropped between them, Tanya became further removed from Stokely's view. Was she really who he thought she was?

"You were pregnant?"

She looked away.

Stokely sat back and exhaled a deep sigh. "You weren't going to tell me? Oh wait, let me guess, you weren't sure if I was the father?"

The rage returned with more intensity.

Pedro stormed away from the bar. A betting man would wager that Pedro had hoped to parlay whatever working relationship he had with Phoenix into something more intimate; but that would have been a sucker's bet. A better wager would have to bet whether his questions of who Stokely was and/or the proximity of Jake caused him to not say the dismissive words that wounded men spew when their approach is rescinded. Nevertheless, Pedro stormed from the restaurant.

Seconds later, he would be followed unknowingly by Stokely who chose to leave Tanya and ten dollars for his drink in the booth before his temper exploded.

Pedro was outside standing in the doorway near the sidewalk attempting to place a call when Stokely stormed by bumping and causing him to drop his phone.

"Motherfucker!" Pedro exclaimed.

Phoenix and Jake were coming through the doorway.

Thankfully, they had taken a moment to pay their tab. That led to the delay that caused Phoenix to see Stokely's right hook go by as opposed to being two steps closer and catching it on the top of her head.

Pedro caught it just under his left eye. The punch caused him to join his phone on the sidewalk. His head took a bounce on the cement and his hostility fled like an escaped prisoner from a chain gang.

Phoenix screamed, "PROFESSOR ROBESON!" While Jake watched stoically as Pedro made his backward descent. Phoenix grabbed Stokely's right arm, tucked it in hers and proceeded to walk Stokely eastbound down Michigan Avenue.

It was a few blocks before she noticed Stokely's more controlled breathing. "Professor Robeson, what happened?" she asked with their arms still locked together.

What she saw in his eyes was a deep, wounded hurt. She assumed correctly that he wouldn't want her to see his cry of frustration, so she clutched his arm tighter and continued walking.

Traffic flowed through the intersection where the old stadium once stood. Perhaps only in this city would a bus going well over the speed limit roar through what could be generously called the tail end of a yellow light.

The bus and the dropping temperatures of the evening sent a chilling gust that made Stokely encircle Phoenix in his arms in a way that's natural to lovers except he seemed to be looking above her. His embrace communicated one thing, but the pain in his eyes and the punch to Pedro wouldn't allow her to get too comfortable. However, while in Stokely's arms, she thought his cologne smelled nice.

Phoenix was able to breathe in a lungful before he spun her out of his embrace and assumed the street side of their east-bound walk.

CHAPTER FOUR

LATER TUESDAY EVENING

"**P**hoenix, I apologize for punching your friend."

Phoenix burst into a fit of laughter surprising Stokely but eventually causing him to cautiously chuckle along.

"I should be thanking you," she explained. "Pedro is such an ass. He's won a few nickel and dime writing awards and he thinks he's Ta-Nehsi Coates or somebody."

She continued, "Jake is the daring stuntman photographer. He finds the most obscure views and can pull an empathy-inducing photo out of the dilapidated. I never see what he sees until he develops the shot. Jake has a gift. But Pedro?"

She went on, "For a quick second I wanted to do like Chris Tucker when he was standing over Debo in *Friday* ..." They looked at each other and with unified, high-pitched voices squealed, "You got knocked the fuck out!"

They shared a hearty laugh as they crossed over the freeway. As the laughter subsided, Stokely relaxed his arm and caught her hand.

They walked a little further, both thankful for a rare mild

winter night before Phoenix asked, "Professor Robeson, where are we going?"

He stopped to face her. He smiled a blushing, boyish smile. "I ... um ... well... the casino? Yeah, the casino."

"The casino? You're a pugilist and a gambler?" Phoenix inquired.

"Oh, no." He laughed, "I'm not a pugilist - Pedro just kind of had it coming, you know mean-mugging me and whatnot. But no, when I came out tonight, I had planned to walk to the casino thinking it easier to catch a cab there than over at Slow's."

She understood. Then paused a moment before asking, "Professor Robeson, was that your girlfriend?"

He bit his lip and in a soft voice replied, "Was."

Phoenix wanted to ask more but decided it to let him go at his own pace. The casino was a couple of blocks away.

After two blocks, Stokely broke the silence, "Phoenix?"

"Yes?"

"Please call me Stokely."

"Like the string beans?"

They burst into another round of laughter. She followed with "You're old enough for your parents to have been impressed with Stokely Carmichael, I get it. Now if you have a brother named Del Monte, I'm going know something," and they laughed even harder.

They were holding hands as they made their way into the casino lobby. Stokely asked, "Where do you live? I mean, like not your address but like proximity so I can guess how much this cab is going to cost."

"I live in Midtown."

Stokely reached in his pocket and retrieved a twenty-dollar bill. He gave her the twenty, "This should cover your fare. If there's change, consider it a tip. If it goes over, well ... maybe I should have walked you further." They laughed again. Knowing that even at the casino, a cab may be reluctant to pick up a black man, they chose to wait inside the lobby doors. When a cab arrived, they shared a parting hug. During the hug, Phoenix's body went stiff. She took a step back and asked with a bit of surprise, "You have a gun?"

Stokely replied in the humblest voice, "Well, I do a lot of walking for someone who lives in the city. I've never had to use it nor do I ever want to. It's just a precaution."

Phoenix studied his eyes for a moment and then smirked as if she understood. Before turning to leave, she said "Talk with you tomorrow? Thanks for the cab fare and I enjoyed our walk." Her smile was electrifying.

He waited for the cab to pull away before walking toward home. It was hard to contain his excitement over the prospect of "Talking tomorrow."

CHAPTER FIVE

MUCH LATER TUESDAY EVENING

Tanya was waiting when he arrived. She wasn't wearing the clothes she wore at Slow's. In fact, she wasn't wearing many clothes at all.

That moment with Tanya sitting on the hand carved wooden throne from the Republic of Benin, would permanently etch itself into Stokely's psyche for the rest of his days. He would probably carry the image into the afterlife, which would be permissible because the Creator understands when we appreciate her work.

Stokely wanted to be angry. Imagine an old water well from which one must pump and prime the handle before water would come through the spigot. Stokely's ego pumped and primed his temper. But like an abandoned well, no amount of priming could facilitate any anger through the spigot.

Tanya's stunning, seductive beauty had rendered Stokely breathless. The sigh that escaped him coincided with a loss of his composure and a short fall back into the wall.

Of the meager attire that accentuated her body it could be

no debate as to whether each piece was carefully selected. The potency of the sight begins with Tanya's very striking physical features. Without heels, she stands an even six feet. She hadn't risen yet, but those three-inch heels will make her a larger than life seductress.

Even a novice connoisseur could deduct from the way she sat that the symmetry of her curves was a godsend. Her curves were evident from the front, the back, the side, above, and below. Many of Stokely's favorite memories were those nights where he would lay in bed with the curtains drawn and a nearly tangible darkness. Tanya would be in the bathroom wrapping her hair, giving herself a facial, and other female pre-bedtime rituals. For some reason or another, there was always something in her purse that caused her to walk from the bathroom into the bedroom. The light from the bathroom would perfectly outline her figure and the sight induced more erections than any pornographic materials could ever do.

When he saw her perched on the throne with those heels and black nylons that go just above the knee and are topped with a band of lace, he knew that he must pay homage to the queen. Like a queen, she held an open bottle of champagne between her legs completing her regal seductiveness with a scepter of bubbly.

It was commendable that Stokely did not slide down the wall due to a spell of faint-headedness. On a regular day, Tanya was beautiful, so on a night with provocative intentions, her beauty was so boundlessly unfair it was like LeBron James playing basketball against a two-year-old.

Due to Tanya's deep mahogany complexion, she had been teased mercilessly as a child. Her mother's emphasis on pride, poise, and posture meant little to her growing up, but it was quite apparent that mom's tutelage took root because as an adult, Tanya was a commanding presence. Simply being herself made insecure women unnerved and men both intimidated and lustful. The teasing she endured as child paled in comparison to the envy she evoked as an adult - a better payback than she ever could have ever wished.

Much to Stokely's disbelief there was no correlation between the numbers of men whose breath had been taken away by Tanya to those who had the confidence to approach her. Besides her mother's words, Tanya felt little affirmation of her beauty from others. She sometimes felt like a spectacle or an object for viewing, but seldom did she feel viewed as someone with whom others would want to develop a long-term relationship. Oscar made her feel like a trophy. On the other hand, Stokely filled a tremendous void within her and her sustaining of their relationship was born out of appreciation primarily and physical and intellectual attraction following second and third. The part of her that was consumed with the future was satiated by Oscar and his ability to provide financial security. But her needs as a woman to be both loved and desired right now were superbly satisfied by Stokely. Which is important considering right now is really all we have.

Right then, she could see that Stokely was hers.

As she stood, her rose colored satin and lace cami fell just above her waistline. The large audible gulp that Stokely swallowed made her feel like an invincible predator ready to pounce upon a susceptible prey. Moreover, she knew he was more than willing to be pounced upon.

Leaving the champagne on the floor, she reached behind her head to undo the band that held her dreads. How she managed to have four dreads above her right eye grow fully grey while the rest of her dreads were a dark chocolate brown matching her skin is anybody's guess. Stokely would often whisper in Tanya's ear, "God took his time when he made you." To which Tanya would follow by playfully kissing him and say, "She took her time." Stokely would happily concur, "Yes. She took her time." After which he would return her kiss.

With her stride, she crossed the room in three steps. Stokely reached for her but in a swift motion she lightly slapped away his reach, recoiled, intertwined her fingers in his, and pinned both his hands to the wall.

She leaned in so close that Stokely was prepared to kiss her but the kiss didn't happen. When he opened his eyes to see the delay she was staring into his eyes. Her eyes were smoky and her breathing was heavy. She cooed just above a whisper, "Don't you miss me, baby?"

More swiftly than her hand slapped his, yet significantly more smoothly and gently, Stokely flipped their position so that her back was against the wall. Their kiss was hungrily intense. Had Stokely wore linen pants, his erection would have ripped through; yet, the denim he wore was being stretched as far as it would give. When Tanya hooked her leg around him, he reached to caress her ass. Among Tanya's numerous attributes, the fact that her wonderful ass was her erogenous zone was the greatest cherry on top in the annals of love making history.

Unlike their previous sessions of intimacy, this go-around didn't make it to the bedroom.

WHAT WOULD BECOME a pile of his clothes on the floor would also be the cushion for their impassioned love making. The fury with which they met each other stroke for stroke couldn't last long and their unified orgasms sent them tottering towards the floor.

For a moment, they lay side to side on their backs gasping for air.

Stokely was still trying to calm his breathing when he could feel the soft velvet-ness of Tanya's inner thigh begin drape along his abdomen. She then traced her fingers along his collarbone only pausing to draw small feathery circles on his Adam's apple. This time, there was no fury just a sensuous familiarity, the sustenance of their relationship.

The sudden vaginal clutch that preceded Tanya's orgasm caused Stokely to ejaculate so hard it was as if they levitated from the floor. By the time, they floated back down in a feathery descent, they were both asleep.

Stokely awakened first. Their bodies were still moist from perspiration. Tanya was snoring and yet snuggled closer as he caressed her ass.

He was truly conflicted. He had been attracted to women before but Tanya drew an animalistic lust from his soul. He loves that, but does he love her? Does she love him? People can't make that kind of love without real love involved. So how in the hell does she just pack-up and leave?

Worry emanated from him and stirred Tanya. She whispered, "Baby, can we talk like two people who love each other?" She really knew how to make him focus.

CHAPTER SIX

WEDNESDAY

"We need to get Iyanla to fix ole Roses' life!" Denise bellowed with laughter as she rounded the last lap of the morning walk with her daughter.

Phoenix and her mother, Denise, are often mistaken for sisters. As a child, Phoenix remembered how people would comment on her mothers' striking resemblance to Chaka Khan. There is no doubt that Chaka is a better singer, but Denise and Chaka both exude effervescent sexiness. Save for her closely cropped, fully grey natural compared to Phoenix's curly twists and Denise's inch and a half height advantage, it is nearly impossible to distinguish mother and daughter apart. The older men who lumbered around the track often experienced warmth pass over their hearts whenever the Ellison duo passed them on the track.

Every Monday, Wednesday, and Friday, mother and daughter meet at the downtown YMCA for a brisk five-mile walk. Individually, they participated in an assortment of spinning, Pilates, swimming, and Zumba classes; yet, three days a week at 7am, they dedicated time to each other. Sometimes they laughed as old friends, other times could find them in simple mother-to-daughter heart-to-heart conversations, and occasionally when they did not talk, they would just hold hands. Denise has always been overtly affectionate and her demonstrative love resonated with and was duplicated by her daughter.

"Mom, when did you know you loved daddy?"

Denise squeezed Phoenix's hand and smiled wistfully. "Your father was the catch at Grambling." Phoenix's parents had both graduated from Grambling State University. Following graduation, Phoenix's father would become an officer in the Army. He was deployed thousands of miles away in Libya when Denise went into labor and in some ways that distance remained throughout his relationship with Phoenix. He would return from Libya a different man than the one with whom her mother fell in love. As a child, she was more accustomed to her father's absence than his presence. In retrospect, it seemed that he endured her more than her enjoyed her. It was as if he were viewing her life from a distance and though making provisions, maintained some minimal semblance of parenting.

Before moving with her mother to Detroit, her father deserted the family. It's amazing that Denise did not harbor bitterness. On more than one occasion she would tell Phoenix "Never waste your time trying to make a man be where his heart isn't."

Never fully answering Phoenix's inquiries about her father, Denise would talk specifically about a certain memory while being protectively non-revealing about much else. This day wasn't much different as they turned the last curve before giving each other a high five and a hug. Denise would proceed to a weightlifting while Phoenix would prepare for a day at the office.

STOKELY AWOKE in the nude about two feet away from an empty champagne bottle. He didn't want to open his eyes because that would confirm that Tanya had gone.

"What a night," he thought. "From the letter under the door, to the restaurant, to knocking Pedro's ass out to Phoenix ..."

The thought of Phoenix opened his eyes.

He gathered himself from the floor. He and Tanya had previously never made love on the floor. She was really trying to get her point across. Such a roller coaster night capped with mind-blowing sex probably ensured for senseless post coitus conversation. Yet, not even a few moments could pass before his thoughts returned to Phoenix.

While gathering his clothes from the floor, he felt Phoenix's card inside his coat pocket. He traced his fingers slowly along the raised ink as if it were braille. He knew then he would visit her office. It was 8:30. The Metropolitan Revitalization Organization interview was at 4:00 - he had plenty of time.

HER OFFICE WAS in Tech Town, a cluster of renovated warehouses financed by the university to facilitate the development of start-up businesses. Stokely took the stairs to the fourth floor where the BBD suite was at the far end of the hall.

While waiting in reception area, what he thought were internal chuckles were audible as Phoenix approached from him behind.

"What's so funny?" she asked with unexpected mirth.

Stokely jumped initially but looked to her and pointed to her business logo on the wall he had been facing. Inside a large heart were the letters B.B.D. representing the abbreviation of her company's name.

Phoenix was puzzled.

Stokely began rapping lines from Phife Dawg's *Electric Relaxation* verse. To which Phoenix followed precisely on cue with Q-Tip's bars. By the time they got to the hook, they both had begun their own 1990s hip hop inspired two-steps. Their impromptu A Tribe Called Quest reenactment was followed by a round of laughter and a friendly hug.

"BBD stands for Building Beautiful Daughters - the name of my nonprofit organization that takes seventh grade girls and mentors them through high school graduation. Our first cohort is now in 11th grade. We're excited about not only expanding their world view, but also preparing them to graduate from college," Phoenix explained.

Stokely was affirmed in his choice to see her. "She's a petite sized dynamo," he thought.

"What about the small publishing company you write for?" Stokely inquired.

Phoenix turned with her arms folded, rapped Jay Z's Michael Jordan line from *Best of Both Worlds* when he spits about playing for the team he owns.

It took Stokely too long to recall the song and by the time recognition dawned upon him, Phoenix was shaking her head.

"I thought you were a real hip hop head," she said with playful sarcasm.

"So, you own the publishing company too?"

"Almost - we're going to launch the company with the first photo book we're developing now. Save for the fact that our best writer got the taste knocked out his mouth, we were making steady progress."

Stokely meekly retorted, "I can write."

Phoenix laughed hard. Stokely was confused. She waved

her hand and while laughing said, "Remember in *Boomerang* when the lady passes them and David Alan Grier says all sheepishly 'I'm from Detroit.'? That's what you sound like."

Stokely almost said, "Fuck you" in the playful way he and his friends joke with each other but thought better of it. He laughed along and replied, "You got jokes, hunh? I was looking to share my talent as a freelance writer and since all the lights in the other offices were out, I stopped in here hoping you could help." She smiled knowing he was mocking her foray into the architecture building the other day.

After the giggles subsided and they took seats in her office, she looked him squarely in the eye, "What brings you here today?"

Without a flinch, he replies, "You."

She leaned back in her chair. While she sifted uncomfortably, he marveled at her office. It felt more like an art studio than an office. The chairs are all of a bar stool height and her desk wasn't a desk at all but a highly-raised glass table with one glass drawer beneath. His inner architect would have taken more time to study the table but a soft thud that caused him to peer through the table and notice she had kicked off her shoes.

Her feet were lovely, which he observed even through the nylon. He allowed his eyes to wander from under the table, up her legs and torso to her face. She watched him with a smirk.

"Let me get this right," Phoenix stated dryly.

Then like a cross examining attorney going in for the kill, she began, "You argue with a woman that 'was' your girlfriend." Accentuating "was" with the air quotations gesture, causing him a slight annoyance.

"Punch my writer in the face because you're mad and some other trivial he-looked-at-me wrong BS. Then have the audacity to visit my office, unannounced, and allude to being interested in me?"

They both let the question linger.

When she leaned forward, she did so with an olive branch of hope, "Professor Robeson, I am truly flattered. But you and her - it's something between y'all that needs to be addressed before you and I could be more than colleagues."

She was fishing but struck a chord in Stokely.

He looked around the office and let his gaze rest on what appeared to be half of a totem pole tucked behind a collection of African drums and other cultural paraphernalia.

He took a deep breath and exhaled slowly through his nose.

"Phoenix?" he paused before continuing. "You can call me Stokely. As far as Tanya ..." His words tailed off. He looked to the floor longer than Bill Withers held that note in *Lovely Day*.

"Tanya ..." he muttered.

He gave up. "You're right. There is something ..." he sighed before finishing, "Between us."

He looked out the window and noticed the sun obstructed behind one large grey cloud. He figured that the mild winter days were over and the usual ice-inducing dreary days would resume. He continued to stare outside.

After a minute, Phoenix broke the silence, "Tanya doesn't seem to care too much for me."

Stokely smirked and replied, "She thinks I moved on to you."

"Have you?"

"Am I allowed to dream?"

"You're allowed to hope."

Stokely grimaced and made a gesture with his left hand as if shooing gnats.

"Hope is for the unprepared."

Their eyes locked again.

Possibly due to her height, Phoenix had grown accustomed to being overlooked both literally and figuratively. She practiced martial arts because she felt the need to be prepared to fight just in case someone thought they could take advantage of her size.

"Just in case" frequently sabotaged her relationships. She over-thought them all. If Stokely knew her better, he would know that her dismissal of Pedro had more to do with her than Pedro being an asshole.

"I would like to share an architect's perspective for your book and maybe even write in place of what's-his-face." Stokely said to break the stalemate.

It was Phoenix's turn to stare out the window. She slid down out of the chair, stepped into her shoes and walked over to the window. To protect herself, she simply avoided getting involved with men. However, she hated how she had backed herself into this lonely corner. She had recently turned 27, was beautiful, educated, committed to helping others and hadn't been in a meaningful relationship since her freshman year in college. At that time, she had fallen hard for a basketball player at a neighboring university. He did not see her in the stands but she saw him wink, point, and otherwise continuously acknowledge one of the pep squad members during a game. It wasn't that the pep squad member was white that unnerved her. It was that at that moment her heart hardened about the trustworthiness of men when she wasn't around.

Maybe this is what happens when a girl lives estranged from her father. Since her father could not or would not protect her, she was hyper-vigilant about protecting herself. In her mind, at the first sign of danger, she would execute a perfect roundhouse kick of her size 5 1/2 shoe to the offender's midsection.

So enraptured in her thoughts, she hadn't noticed Stokely standing behind her. He reached and very softly touched her shoulder.

"If my being here makes you uncomfortable, I'll leave."

She pulled away from his touch but turned to face him with puppy eyes. He swallowed hard. "Phoenix ... I won't hurt you."

She turned back toward the window. A few seconds passed and she regained her professional poise. "Professor Robeson, Jake and I will be going over the shots from yesterday pretty soon. Can I call you so that you can join us?"

Stokely backed away. "Sure, call me anytime." With that he turned to leave. As he reached for the door, she called, "Stokely, handle your business with Tanya. I don't know what happened but I do know it's not over. When you're sure it's over, then maybe," she paused and looked to the floor before returning to his gaze, "... you won't have to hope."

CHAPTER SEVEN

WEDNESDAY AFTERNOON

Stokely arrived at the Guardian Building at 3:30. The interview was on the 40th floor. He figured he would take the stairs down as opposed to working up a sweat by taking the stairs up before the interview. The anticipation about the interview had his heart beating faster than a Art Blakey drum solo.

"Welcome to the Metropolitan Revitalization Organization Mr. Robeson, the team will meet with you shortly," the receptionist cooed.

She was pretty. It was easy to discern that forty something years ago, during her prime, she turned plenty of heads. Truth be told, she's still turning heads. Her carriage was like that of a dancer. Stokely wondered if she knew he was looking at her as she made her way back to the desk. When she turned to sit, her flirtatious smile confirmed Stokely's hunch. "Grandmama got it going on," Stokely thought.

"Professor Robeson," Dean Griffin beckoned for Stokely to enter to conference room.

The room was expansive. Its dimensions belied a casual

approximation regarding the width of the building. After a few moments, Stokely deduced that the ceiling was 20 feet high or that it was a two-story room. The crown molding and wooden columns were camel thorn - which considering the scarcity of that kind of wood, conveyed that this organization was very wealthy. Tucked within the crown molding was exquisite lighting. Two walls consisted of very large windows. Stokely didn't know drapes but imagined his mother would squeal with near orgasmic delight had she had an opportunity to brush her cheeks along the fabric of the drapes in this room.

Dean Griffin commenced with an introduction of the trio representing the Metropolitan Revitalization Organization. At a glance, the trio consisted of a Middle Eastern guy, a white guy, and one of the Black dudes who the old folk would say could "pass."

"Professor Robeson, please meet Mr. Anwar Hassan, Mr. Isadore Bernstein, and Mr. Oscar Rousseau the third."

Stokely managed to keep his jaw from dropping but his heart sank all forty stories to the lobby. He shook each of the outstretched hands and sat in the chair Dean Griffin had pulled for him.

As soon as they sat, Mr. Bernstein began, "Aaaah, Mr. Robeson, John speaks very highly of you."

It was hard not to stare or hurry old Isadore along. Rather quickly, Stokely calculated that he was in his 90s and had to wind up before each sentence.

"Aaaaaahhh, the Metropolitan Revitalization Organization began in 1952 as a very exclusive collection of men committed to Detroit's well-being." Stokely imagined that this was the point when Isadore would reach for his inhaler, but instead Bernstein pressed forward. "Aaaaaahhhhh, you can imagine the grave disappointment we feel about the city's current state. We have a vision, a means to chart this city toward a more family friendly community."

"Aaaaaaaaaahh, have you ever been to Portland, Robeson?"

Stokely replied that he hadn't. Bernstein looked over to Rousseau and said, "Aaaaaaah, Ossie, we must get Robeson to Portland." He turned to face Stokely and continued, "Aaaaahh, the City of Roses is indeed a beautifully splendid place."

Stokely was unsure where the conversation was headed but listened intently while quietly hoping that Bernstein would not ask ole Ossie boy to fetch tea.

"Aaaaaaah, we want people to feel that way about to Detroit. We want people to marvel at our city and dream of ways they can return and stay."

"I agree," Stokely said anxiously but Dean Griffin's slight head gesture conveyed a subtle shut-up-and-listen cue. To which Stokely obliged. "Aaaaaaaaaahh, we are planning for more walkway and jogging spaces and want to begin ..." At that point, Isadore begin a fitful coughing spree. Anwar never took his stare from Stokely, but Oscar looked to Dean Griffin and asked, "Can you get Edna in here?"

Dean Griffin left and within seconds returned with the receptionist. The way her fingers ran over Isadore's shoulder and down his back was sensuously familiar. "Issy, let's get you some rest," she murmured. Edna probably would've made Nichelle Nichols jealous with her well-preserved beauty and Stokely assumed that preservation may be funded by and enjoyed by Isadore Bernstein. There was no panic in her movements as she helped him to his feet. For them, this was routine.

What followed was not routine.

"Gentlemen, could you allow me a few moments with Mr. Robeson?" Rousseau said in an asking tone, but it was more of a directive. Dean Griffin patted Stokely on the back as he rose to leave. Anwar extended a firm handshake with what in his case would be a smile but for anyone else could qualify as a sneer. Mr. Hassan said with a thick Arabic accent, "We look forward to your work Mr. Robeson," and departed with Dean Griffin. They resumed a golfing conversation from earlier as they closed the door behind them.

Stokely and Oscar looked each other in the eye for some time as if they were reading each other. For the first time, Stokely could hear the ticking of the grandfather clock on the other side of the room.

They said nothing. It was a stupid match of egos - a futile case of you-go-first.

Oscar let out a deep sigh, crossed his legs, and then reached for his tortoise shelled glasses. He puffed two breaths onto the lens, polished the glasses with a handkerchief, set them down on the table, and then blew his nose with the same handkerchief. After retrieving his glasses from the table, returning them to his face, and placing his handkerchief in his pocket, he crossed his left leg over his right and folded his hands on his knee.

Stokely observed.

"So, Professor Robeson, we finally have an opportunity to converse," Oscar said after getting settled.

Stokely was at a loss for what to do or say.

"Perhaps you should treat this as any other conversation with a prospective employer save for the facts that you are residing in an apartment for which the prospective employer has paid the lease while having intimate relations with the prospective employer's wife," Oscar said with sarcasm so potent hanging from the last phrase, it was akin to seaweed on an oar.

Stokely's speechlessness endured. He wondered if Oscar was for real or all bluff and bluster. He and Tanya very seldom talked of Oscar. Except for placing him between 55 to his early 60s and knowing that he was a connected millionaire, Stokely knew next to nothing. A part of his inner fiber - particularly the part shaped by his childhood experiences near, on, and around Seven Mile Road - convinced him that he could kick Oscar's ass. Then again, punching Pedro was an anomaly not a norm. Plus, kicking Oscar's ass was bound to have long lasting repercussions. So in lieu of his options, he was going to have to take this moment to the chin.

"Would you prefer that I call you Professor Robeson, Mr. Robeson, or Stokely?"

"Mr. Robeson would suffice."

"You know my wife speaks very fondly of you. You have rendered her quite smitten."

To which Stokely mumbled, "I try my best."

After a brief, stunned silence, Oscar let loose a bellowing hearty laugh. He slapped his knee several times and eventually reached for his handkerchief again. He blew his nose with intermittent guffaws and slapped his leg once more for good measure.

"Tanya never mentioned you were a comedian."

The opportunity with the MRO was the type of break for which Stokely had longed; however, the thought of working with his girlfriend's husband had never been a part of his aspirations. In a spirit of testicular fortitude, Stokely stated with a polite firmness, "The redevelopment plan is one that I can do well. Our conversation about Tanya is one I choose not to have. The circumstances that created the opportunity for she and I to come together - that's between you and her. She moved out of our apartment and out of my life. I choose not to talk about it any further with you."

Stokely felt his opportunity dissipating like water droplets on a hot skillet.

Oscar was taken aback. His lips tightened and his breathing was deliberate. After a few moments passed, he flattened his palm on the table and patted it twice. He exhaled a deep sigh, stood, and said very dryly, "John will provide you with the specifics. Welcome to the Metropolitan Revitalization Organization."

Stokely did not exhale until seconds after he heard the door close. He looked out the window to the darkening Detroit skyline. He wasn't sure to be happy or angry. But damn sure that he wasn't going to allow his past to mess up his future, at least not without a fight.

CHAPTER EIGHT

WEDNESDAY EVENING

After settling in their first-class seats, Tanya looked at the side of Oscar's face and asked, "Are you happy now?" The question lingered for a moment as he leaned his head back and exhaled a pained sigh. He slowly turned to his right to face her.

She was as beautiful as she had always been. Their years of marriage had aged him tremendously but she was as spry as the first time they met. Even in grief, as he assumed she was grieving the abrupt ending to her dalliance with Stokely, she exuded regality.

When he looked into her eyes, small daggers of disappointment and embarrassment channeled through his vision. He had left his family for her. At that time, he envisioned a relationship modeled after Isadore and Edna.

He closed his eyes and shook his head when he thought of Edna. He and Edna had been lovers. His Puritan approach to lovemaking was no match for her toppling-of-furniture tenacity. He knew he couldn't keep up but certainly relished trying.

Moreover, remembering Edna led him to thinking that this thing with Stokely was a bad turn of karma.

When he opened his eyes, Tanya had turned away.

He chuckled when thinking of the irony that Isadore had known of his and Edna's trysts all along. Edna eventually confided in him that it had been Isadore's prompting that pushed her to come onto him. The difference between now and then was that Isadore had been a widower and as Edna explained, impotent. Edna was Isadore's company, a lady friend for a lonely man. However, Oscar was married to Tanya and capable of having sex every other Saturday night. He did not foresee that residing in two different cities equated to living two different lives.

Tanya could see the city lights of Detroit fading as the airplane continued to ascend. She missed Stokely more than she anticipated. Her thoughts drifted to memories of how on a night like tonight, Stokely's head would be resting on her bare thighs as he took playful swipes at her dangling locs like a frisky kitten.

She shifted her weight and moved her body toward the window. She knew Oscar knew she was thinking of Stokely but she didn't care. Since her body couldn't be with him, she wanted to enjoy the memories of him. She thought dolefully about how Stokely convinced her of the comforts of boy shorts. She recalled that once he bought her a pair, those and the others she eventually bought became her at-home-after work attire. Which to Stokely's delight, showcased the splendor of her hips and ass. More often than not, his view of her in those shorts was more than an aphrodisiac for him and enticed him to reach for and commence to rubbing and caressing her behind. Kissing would ensue and ... and ... Her thoughts were so vivid; she could nearly feel his hands caressing her ass even as she sat on this flight with her husband.

"Damn, I miss my man!" she thought.

As the lights of Detroit gave way to a starless darkness, one disappointing thought gave way to another, "How am I going to make this every other Saturday sex work?"

~

HAD the MRO interview occurred a week earlier, Stokely would have rushed home with the good news. Or would he? There is no truthful retelling of the interview without including Oscar and the ensuing awkwardness.

Now here he was on his fourth Guinness and second order of chicken wings at Flood's Bar & Grille. How can a circumstance that would seem to be celebratory have such a dampening cloud affixed to it? These last few days were a roller coaster with no apparent end.

From his corner perch at the bar, Stokely had an unobstructed view of the dance floor. Usually, he met the fellas at Flood's for their midweek eye-candy-surveying-shit-talking sessions, but Terrence was out of reach (his availability was always a 50/50 chance), Stephen was at home doctoring his sick son, and Wes was clocking some overtime hours. They would have enjoyed tonight's view.

The small band, Gina's Groove, was doing an exceptional rendition of the Incognito catalog. Regina was the singer but preferred to be called Gina. Her legs were so shapely, Tina Turner would be outdone. Gina sashayed around the minuscule stage with much more effervescence than one would expect from a midweek bar & grille band. Rumor has it that she is a middle school teacher; Stokely sort of chuckled at the thought of having a teacher with legs like that. That would have certainly been his perfect attendance class.

The band fed off the energy of the three sisters on the dance floor. One had a collection of singles, fives, and other dollar denominations safety-pinned to her dress. Although it was too cold for a shoulders-out, strapless dress, the woman was enjoying her birthday. If he thought about it hard enough, Stokely would have recognized that the birthday girl was trying to out-gyrate Gina. The band recognized it as they seemed to play more of Incognito's up-tempo pieces to feed the energy. Gina damn sure recognized it as she worked her hips even harder.

When the drummer began the solo from *Hold on To Me*, Gina put one foot up on the speaker and the split in her skirt allowed the material to unveil her beautifully muscular thigh.

Stokely coughed up the chicken he was chewing. But the drummer's enthusiasm spurred an ass-swinging frenzy from the birthday girl that caught everyone's attention. Both the gentleman being patted-down in the entrance and the mountainous security guard stopped to acknowledge this audacious display of derrières-in-motion. Both of the birthday girl's friends were dropping it like it's hot and shaking it like salt shakers; but when the birthday girl grabbed hold of the top of dress, bent over, and alternated wiggling one butt cheek at a time before dropping into a full split every man and the one lesbian with a view of the dance floor mouthed "Gotdamn!" Even Gina chimed "Get it girl!" into the mic. The fellas would hate that they missed this night.

As head nods were exchanged around the bar in appreciation of what they witnessed, Stokely's thoughts returned to Phoenix. He wanted to share his good news with someone but when the replay of their last encounter came to mind; he dismissed the thought of telling her but not the thought of her. He figured that she would have been good company at the bar tonight. She laughs easily and accentuates those laughs with her beautiful smile. The thought of sitting at a bar stool reminded him of her office, which led to thoughts of her mentoring company, and her book publishing goals. The smile that began to stretch across his face was interrupted by Gina.

"All that ass makes you smile?"

With a swift motion of his napkin to cover his mouth, Stokely's eyes flew open in innocence and he shook his head in a vigorous "No" motion that was so childish looking it caused Gina to laugh. The combination of embarrassment and hot sauce caused sweat to break across his forehead as Gina leaned over to the bartender and asked, "Can you make my tea a little hotter and squeeze some lemon into it too?"

Stokely was trying to finish chewing when she turned to him and with a gentle poking of her index finger into his hand said, "And you need to stop looking at me with those eyes of yours. You make a woman feel like you really want her the way you look at her."

The questions in Stokely's mind caused his brow to furrow. Gina placed her right hand on his face and said, "You got the nerve to blush after getting me all bothered." She laughed at her own punch line.

By the time Stokely finished chewing, Gina had turned to the bartender, reached for the tea mug, and said, "Thank you darling." Only God knows how someone can gulp down an entire mug of hot tea in one long swallow, but Gina did it. When she finished, she turned to a shocked Stokely, placed a hand on his knee and asked, "Are you staying for our next set?"

In his first opportunity to say something, he stuttered, "I'mma, I, I think so. Yeah, I love good music." She laughed, patted his thigh, squeezed it, and said, "Umph, that's good. I'll sing something for you." Her smile was casually devious and her eyes were flirtatiously electric. She missed the transformation of dark brown man turning crimson when a friend of hers drunkenly bawled, "GINA GIRL, YOU WAS SANGING DEM DAMN SONGS!!" Gina turned to cheerfully embrace her friend while Stokely exhaled a long sigh. He really had to piss after all those beers, but with such an intense erection he'd knock over everyone on his way to the restroom. The thought took him back to middle school when he was slouching down in his seat and his knee brushed Kellie's behind. He remembered using his Trapper Keeper folder to cover his erection as the bell rang for them to change classes. But on this night, with no Trapper Keeper, he would have to sit uncomfortably with a full bladder and a full erection until things calmed down or Gina stopped bumping her behind on his leg as she talked to her friend.

CHAPTER NINE

LATE WEDNESDAY EVENING

Tanya stormed ahead like a spoiled child and Oscar followed like an overwhelmed parent. By the time valet retrieved his white Lincoln Navigator, Tanya was nearly in tears. As Oscar sat in the driver's seat, Tanya, with tears streaming down her face, told him sternly, "I deserve your anger but asking me to quit my job is ridiculous. Just who in the hell do you think you are?"

Oscar said nothing. Instead, he shifted into drive and pulled away from the curb. The ride to their Belle Meade estate was silent save for Tanya's occasional sobs.

STOKELY WAS in for a different kind of ride. He stayed for the band's next set which prominently featured Sade. During her rendition of *Sweetest Taboo*, Gina chose to work the audience. As she made her way back to the bandstand, Stokely felt her fingertips touch his spine, trace around his neck and along his jawline. When he swiveled in the chair, she stepped between his knees with smoky eyes, and sang or perhaps purred seductively about how this quiet storm felt unlike others. When she sang the "ooooooooo" in taboo, she flicked a come-hither finger stroke under Stokely's chin which made him lean forward like a mesmerized cartoon.

Gina winked as she made her way back to the stage. An older gentleman with too much cologne and a Bluetooth in his ear leaned over to Stokely and said, "Young blood if you don't handle that, I'll take care of it fa' ya'." Stokely nodded and responded more to himself than the old player, "Nah, I got this."

ONCE IN THEIR GARAGE, Oscar stilled the engine and whispered, "Why do you even want a job? You don't have to work. We have enough money."

Tanya snarled, "YOU have enough money. I like earning my own money." Oscar attempted to talk around his fear of her working in Detroit which to him was synonymous with her affair, "There are plenty of jobs in Nashville; you do not need to go to Detroit to prove anything to me."

Tanya was appalled. "Who said I wanted to prove anything to you? My career is for me. I earned it, went to school for it and sacrificed for it ..." Oscar cut her off, "And threw it away on some young punk!" The word, "punk" echoed in the cabin of the vehicle. They both glared out the window. Both knew that additional verbiage would be cutting and hurtful. They also knew that communication is a preliminary step towards working past this trouble. There was so much to be said; yet between them, they knew that at least now, those things were better left unsaid.

GINA TOSSED the keys to her red Cadillac CTS Coupe to Stokely as if he were her valet. He walked around the passenger side and opened the door for her. Her car was parked in front of Flood's and the collection of security guards, wannabe players, cool cats, and other men gave Stokely a head nod regarding his opportunity to experience Gina's groove.

As they pulled away from the curb, Gina pushed the OnStar button on the rearview mirror and provided an address in Farmington Hills. They turned onto the service drive headed toward Jefferson Avenue. At the light, Gina told Stokely to pull down his pants. The question mark that emerged on Stokely's face was met with a glare from Gina. He unbuckled his belt, unfastened and unzipped his pants, stuck his thumbs into the waistband of both his pants and boxers, and pulled them down to his knees. The leather was cold, but that would soon be of little consequence. Gina leaned across the seat and ...

"Make a right turn onto Jefferson Avenue," OnStar ordered.

Stokely slowly turned the car. Farmington Hills was at least thirty minutes away. As her moans become more audible, he placed his hand on her shoulder and enjoyed the drive.

AFTER TWO GLASSES OF WINE, Tanya moved to the guest room. Oscar had hoped to break the every other Saturday sex cycle and even purchased new lingerie with the hope of some makeup sex. He waited alone in the bed with the untouched gift box. He reached under sheets and thought to pleasure himself. But the tension within their home undermined his attempts at self-arousal.

STOKELY WAS proud that he lasted the entire drive without crashing. The CTS could really move and even at speeds over 75 mph, the handling was superb. For the last few miles, Gina had leaned back against the passenger window, placed one foot on the dashboard, and began pleasing herself. When they arrived at her condo they pulled into a parking space under the building. By the time Stokely parked, she had fetched a condom and crowned him with it. Making love in the driver seat of a coupe is more of an ego boosting, check-it-off-the-bucket-list thing than it is a regular experience, but Stokely was determined to give Gina something that's taboo.

CHAPTER TEN

THURSDAY MORNING

P hoenix felt compelled to make two phone calls. Both were challenging calls to make. One of the calls would help her make sense of where she had been and the other could possibly be a light towards where she was going.

After numerous requests, Denise had finally given Phoenix a number with which she could call her father - a call she considered the most difficult of her life. The difficulty of that call had a discouraging effect on the other call. Instead of the other call, she emailed:

GOOD MORNING PROFESSOR ROBESON,

I am happy that you are considering lending your architectural perspective and possible writing talents to our project. Jake and I will meet at 5:00 this afternoon at Union Street to review photographs and plan some next steps for this venture. Hopefully, you can join us.

PHOENIX Ellison
   President, Building Beautiful Daughters, Inc.

> *"The true worth of a race must be measured*
> *by the character of its women."*
> ~ *Mary McLeod Bethune* ~

SHE LINGERED for several moments before hitting send. She pondered the professional tone. She wondered was there enough hope or whatever embedded within the message that could make Stokely know that not only was she interested in him but also, she wanted that interest to grow. She wasn't sure if he could write at all; but if the book is a vehicle for them to interact; she felt she needed to leverage it. Plus, she already had Jake's pictures and his good luck note that mentioned he would be unable to freelance on this project. Without a writer and a photographer, her book dream had been dealt two Mike Tyson type blows to the gut. Discouragement was becoming her steady friend.

THE CAB COST $45.00, but after a night like last night, Stokely would happily pay that fare anytime. Love making in the car had only been a prologue. Gina's sexual appetite was voracious. It was if she had been pent-up or holding back for years and finally released the floodgates. From her conversation over breakfast, Stokely gathered she was a single mother who was acutely sensitive about dating or her six-year-old son seeing her with different men. Her retired mother kept Gina's son,

Malcolm, on the nights she sang with the band. She explained that between being a mother, her teaching job, and the band, she hardly has any time to date. She went on about hoping he didn't think she was some kind of freak, it was just that her needs were so dang-on pressing that way he looked at her singing with those dreamy eyes just put her over the edge.

Stokely listened and understood. But deep down, he hoped she did not want a good-bye quickie because she had literally tapped him out. He would need a day or two to recover from last night. His testicles were throbbing from overuse. That last ejaculation rendered no fluid. Between the previous night with Tanya and last night with Gina, he was spent.

The more Gina talked, the more she cooked. It had been a minute since Stokely had a home cooked breakfast and Gina certainly satisfied that longing. She looks wonderful, can cook, sings, and brings the thunder sexually? "Ssssshhhhheeeeeiiii-ittttttt!" Stokely thought, "She could be Mrs. Robeson."

However, despite all of Gina's advantages, he was trying to heal from the hurt caused by Tanya and more than that, he longed to see Phoenix.

HIS THOUGHTS of Phoenix carried him up the stairway to the 16th floor of his apartment building. So consuming were his thoughts of Phoenix, the sound of her name echoed in his footsteps as he climbed the stairs. Thoughts of her stayed with him as he entered the nearly empty apartment. Those thoughts were interrupted as he passed the empty champagne bottle. Yet, when his eyes fell upon the hand carved throne, he paused in silent homage to the image of Tanya sitting there the night before. The tribute prompted a tingling in his crotch. If there was champagne left in the bottle, he would have poured out a little liquor to the memory.

Just as surely as he left the room, his thoughts returned to Phoenix. As he undressed to shower, he wondered when he would see her again.

~

OSCAR AROSE to a note printed on parchment paper which read:

OSCAR,
   I love you.
   I am also not in love with you.
   Loving you is sweet, for you are a remarkable man.
   Not being in love with you happened over time.
   In the beginning, your ability to provide all my wants and needs made me feel secure in our relationship. Overtime I began to feel like an accomplishment or accessory of yours. During that same time, a growing part of me wanted to define my life on my own terms.
   Do you know how many African American women hold a Ph.D. in engineering? Very few, in fact too few. How can I be blessed with such an opportunity and allow it to atrophy while I waltz around as a domestic showpiece? Doesn't that disrespect the opportunity, the sacrifices, and the women I'm responsible for bringing along? I have accountability to my sisters, my profession, and myself to do more with the fortune of which I've been blessed to experience.
   That is the easy part.
   Now the hard part - I did not plan to have an affair. I could elaborate about Stokely, but essentially, especially as it relates to you, the responsibility is mine. Years ago, before my mother

passed, she warned me that if I were to ever marry, she said, "Don't leave no loop holes in y'all's relationship." I never knew what she meant but now I understand more clearly. In addition to feeling like an accessory, our regimented sex life left some loop holes in my emotional needs. I did not know that then but I know it now.

Right now, I am an emotional wreck. For all the assorted feelings I feel, there is one of which I am most certain - I am not quitting my job. I plan to return to Detroit. For our sake, I will put in a transfer request to Nashville. I do not know if such an opportunity exists but I will try. I will also stay at a hotel instead of the apartment.

Right now, that's all I can promise besides being more intentional with honest communication.

YOUR WIFE,
  Tanya

OSCAR REREAD the letter three times. He resigned to thinking if this was a first step toward healing, he would take it. But he was worse than unhappy about her return to Detroit. Getting her a job in Nashville is a one phone call matter for him. Yet, he knew she would vehemently oppose any assistance from him regarding her career. The notion prompted him to lament, "Why did she have to be so difficult?"

CHAPTER ELEVEN

THURSDAY AFTERNOON

ARC 312 - *Experiencing Architecture Studio* could easily become Stokely's favorite class. The students who chose architecture because they like to draw have been weeded out and those who have made it to this class are committed visionaries. Speaking of commitment, Stokely is committed to teaching this class so effectively, that even if Dr. Coleman returns from sabbatical there is no way he gets it back.

The giddiness of teaching genuine learners carried him back to his office. There his officemate took one look at him and swore, "Robeson looks like you're in love there, yessir, you're in love." Stokely was surprised, but laughed appreciatively as he sat at his desk. He turned on his computer and spoke to his office mate over his shoulder, "I just left a class with students who really want to learn!" The office mate mumbled an "Mmmmm-hmmmm" to sound interested but he had already begun to drift into one of the numerous naps he would take that day.

Phoenix's email was the first and only email Stokely read. It struck him in a myriad of ways. First, he would meet Phoenix and Jake to discuss the photo book project. Any opportunity to meet with and talk to Phoenix was an opportunity he was determined to maximize. But there seemed like something else she was trying to say. Since the meeting in her office, he had resigned to just being Professor Robeson to her, although he had his fingers crossed that he wouldn't always be confined to that role. She was on to something about Tanya, except in his mind the matter was proceeding through the grief of what was, not some magical reconciliation. Phoenix didn't know Tanya was married and Stokely had long accepted that being involved with a married woman could have an unhappy ending. Life with Tanya was so good that the journey was well worth the heartbreak he knew he would eventually suffer.

"What time are you heading home?" Stokely asked, but when he turned and saw his office mate with his hands folded atop his stomach, head back, and mouth open, he knew better than to expect a response. If this were middle school, Stokely would launch a few spit balls into his partner's mouth, but he decided against the temptation. He packed his things, checked the clock that read 4:35, turned off the light, and pulled the door nearly closed. On his way out he heard a muffled, "Yessir Robeson is in love, in love ..." A quick snort confirmed he had resumed his nap.

Given the proximity to Union Street, he opted to walk while leaving his truck securely parked in the staff parking structure. Who knows? Maybe Phoenix has a car and could give him a ride back. The thought of being alone with Phoenix made him smile, even if alone was a five-minute car ride. The light snow that had begun to fall couldn't chill the warmth Phoenix brought to his heart.

∽

AS STOKELY EXITED the architecture building, Tanya was checking into the Marriott in the Renaissance Center downtown. She was bothered that Oscar had hired movers to gather her things from the apartment. She was certain they must have mixed some of Stokely's belongings with hers. With most her wardrobe in transit to Nashville, she had to rent a car at the airport, drive all the way to the Nordstrom's at Twelve Oaks Mall to purchase some suits, casual wear, stockings, shoes, boots, underwear, loungewear, and perfume. While making the drive to downtown Detroit, she thought that even though her shopping spree was fueled by a vindictive spirit, the matter would be of little consequence to Oscar. He would pay the balance in full no matter the amount.

She rented a blue Chrysler 300 with all the bells and whistles. She felt a sense of pride driving a vehicle she helped design. In addition to enjoying the ride, she reflected on the last few days. She had called-in for a few personal days when she learned Oscar was in town. But now she looked forward to returning to the office in Auburn Hills. Work would be a welcomed distraction from the emotional tumult she had undergone in the last few days. Tomorrow after work, she planned for another shopping spree at the Somerset Collection. She was going to have to stay busy if she was going to avoid the temptation of reaching out to Stokely. Deep down, she knew that it was only a matter of time. She loves Stokely and although her actions probably said so, she realized she hadn't said so. She had allowed something that mattered so much, to go unsaid.

PHOENIX WAS SEATED in the rear with photographs spread over the table. Stokely wouldn't have known that she was watching the door while attempting to appear casual. She waved when he entered. As he made his way toward the table, she used the time to admire his handsomeness and physique. His boyish face contradicted his age so much so that one had to be deep into conversation with him before gauging approximately how old he was. She was enamored by chocolate skin and inviting brown eyes. Physically, he moved with a muscular grace that spoke of athletic experience. When he reached the table, she stood to shake his hand. Instead, he engulfed her in a full embrace. The part of her that wanted to maintain the professional facade wanted to push away. However, the woman who spent more nights alone than she liked, felt comforted in his arms. The scent of his cologne accented what was a fulfilling, if all too brief of a moment.

"I hope Jake makes it safely in this weather. The snow is turning to sleet," Stokely said. He looked to the door as if Jake would enter at that moment. The moment found Phoenix conflicted - should she tell him the truth or lie?

"I don't think Jake's going to make it," she said more timidly than she intended. Stokely turned and looked out the window while asking, "Did he say he wasn't coming?" Phoenix's sigh cued Stokely that he should not inquire about Jake again. As he focused on Phoenix, he noticed that she wore little make up but her skin was resplendently radiant. "Wow, even in the winter?" he thought. She had on one of those big scarves that ladies and guys who are trying to be trendy wear. When she adjusted it, her fragrance filled the air causing Stokely to practice restraint to keep from sniffing the air like a puppy in the kitchen when dinner is being prepared. To keep his composure, he focused on Phoenix. When she smiles it's as if her cheeks point upward toward her earrings. Some would consider her smile more of a passionate blush of someone who if nudged would happily reveal some spectacular news.

They sat there exchanging smiles, blushes, and glances to the floor or the window.

AROUND THAT SAME TIME, Tanya sat stranded on south-bound I-75. After trying to catch up at work, she was physically drained. Now stuck on an increasingly slippery highway facing the onset of nighttime and plummeting temperatures, Tanya had an epiphany or two. Despite her anger at his ultimatum to quit her job, she loved Oscar. She realized that her time with Stokely should end. Stokely was a wonderful young man, but there were many parts of life's journey that he would have to face where she would not want to accompany him. Oscar's age, he was nearly 15 years her senior, brought a certain stability with it - a stability that buoyed her professional drive. She could afford to be cutting edge and push the envelope at work because she didn't have to work. That professional edginess brought her tremendous satisfaction.

She had already talked with human resources about transferring to the Nashville area. All the current opportunities would be steps backward. In the meantime, she signed a lease for a small townhouse closer to the office. This commute to Detroit was senseless if she was not going to her and Stokely's love nest. To her, Detroit equaled Stokely, if she was going to move forward without him, as challenging as that may be, she was going to have to leave Detroit. She didn't know when she'd speak to Oscar because she had full intentions of riding out this wave of anger toward him; yet, as a sign of her softening position, she was excited to tell him about her new place and her appreciation for the gift he sent. With a different type of excited anticipation, she knew she should talk with Stokely soon. She needed closure.

CHAPTER TWELVE

EARLY THURSDAY EVENING

Jake's pictures were captivating. Particularly the one he took of a hallway that captured a setting sun through a windowless and broken window frame. The picture was bordered by debris and graffiti along the corridor walls. Just beyond the window frame were leafless tree branches along with rooftops, some caved, others burned, and a handful still intact. But the setting sun steals the picture and added nuanced texture to Phoenix's photo book.

"That has to be the cover," Stokely suggested as he slid the 8 1/2 by 11 across the table to Phoenix.

"I agree." Phoenix replied, "Jake really captured the tone I wanted. I just hate that he can't go forward with us."

"Dammit! I did not want to tell him yet," she thought.

Stokely sensing some type of discomfort from Phoenix made an attempt at optimism, "I'm sure he has his reasons, but that doesn't stop your plans for the book, does it?"

Phoenix, slightly but happily taken aback, responded, "No, it just sort of slows things down a bit. In just a few days I've lost a writer and photographer ..." Before she could finish, Stokely inserted, "And gained an architect and hopefully a good friend." The smile that followed his comment made Phoenix blush more. They were looking at each other warmly when the waitress interrupted.

"Hey Phoenix!" then she turned to face Stokely. "Welcome to Union Street, my name is Hannah and I'll be your server tonight. Phoenix, honey, I like the pullback look on you! Do you want to start with the usual Corona with a lime?"

Phoenix smiled and said. "Thanks Hannah! And you know it!"

"Sir, what drink would you like start you off with?"

"I'll have one of those Angry Orchard Ciders."

"Alrighty, I'll be back in a minute with your drinks."

As Stokely turned back to Phoenix and kicked himself for having not complimented her on her hair before Hannah, he missed Hannah standing a few feet behind him mouthing "He's cute" and giving Phoenix two thumbs up. Phoenix chuckled.

Stokely's doubt, Hannah's gestures, and Phoenix's chuckle transpired in a matter of seconds; what was taking much longer was for traffic to resume moving on I75.

IN THE STILLNESS of her car with the radio off and the soft descent of a snow and sleet mix making music of its own on the car, Tanya was becoming overwhelmed by the fragrant roses on the passenger seat. Oscar surprised her with the bouquet waiting at her desk by the time she arrived in her office. She wanted to be ungrateful but the initial tough girl sarcastic thought, "He could have shipped my car back instead," rang painfully hollow. Without the roses, this traffic would have caused her to scream but instead she was reminded of Oscar's giving spirit. It helped counter the memory of last winter, when she was sitting in similar circumstances. After phoning Stokely about the predicament, he showed up forty-five minutes later after exiting a cab on the freeway's service drive, sliding down the embankment onto the freeway, and waltzing though the other stranded cars with a bag of coneys. They had a coney dinner in the car. What was funny is that in all his clever sweetness, he only brought one drink and no napkins! Then had the audacity to suggest, "Sip, sip, give."

Just as she recalled wiping mustard on his jeans, traffic began to move slowly in her memory and in real time. Yes, she was going to make it work with Oscar but knew she would hold her memories of Stokely dear to her heart.

THEY EYED each other playfully behind the humongous mound of chicken and cheese nacho chips. Having bit into a juicy jalapeño, Stokely gasped for relief and downed what remained of his cider. Phoenix laughed heartily. Between nacho chips, they talked about how things were bad but had gotten considerably worse after Kwame. "Kwame" referred to the former mayor, Kwame Kilpatrick. They agreed that there were some covert factions relishing the opportunities Kwame provided for them to exploit his character flaws. Phoenix proclaimed, "That if the lynch mob is after you don't hand their asses the rope!"

Ask any Detroiter about Mayor Kilpatrick and surely his story evokes within them a story of their own. For Stokely, the story was one of admiration that evolved into a clearer understanding of the adage about giving young people too much power too soon. He was an architect in one of those firms that had been ostracized from opportunities because of the business practices employed by the Kilpatrick administration. He cheered for and despised the brother simultaneously.

Phoenix's story reflected great empathy for Kwame's wife and his mistress. The women that Stokely knew tended to take one side or another, but Phoenix had a heart for them both. Then a conversation point was punctuated with the rhetorical question "What kind of man sleeps with married women?" Stokely grimaced hard. Phoenix did not stop talking but made a mental note of his brief display of discomfort.

She also noted how Stokely veered the conversation another way when he asked a rhetorical question of his own, "Then what did Bing do when he got in office? Diddly squat, that's what"

Now if the conversation were about Detroit, then Stokely's comment would have fit the flow. But Phoenix thought they were discussing Kwame and the effects of his choices. If that was indeed the conversation, then Stokely's comments were random at best, direction-altering at worse. She knew that in dating, she tended to overthink things. She made a quick promise not to forget but not to dwell on it unless other matters corroborated it. Moreover, in what has been an otherwise enjoyable night, she chose to be present as opposed to shackling her fears with speculation. Confirmation of her choice was the smile that emerged on her face.

The smile perfectly coincided with the compliment that followed Stokely's remarks, "Is it really Bing's fault? I mean whether it's Black people, Americans, or Western society it seems like there is this misguided norm that wholesale changes will be led by one extraordinary person. Nah, it is going to take contributions from many exceptionally dedicated people who appear ordinary but are invested in change. Like you and what you are doing with those girls ..." He saw her smile. He hoped that she grasped his sincerity and not mistake his words for charm.

"You should join us - me and the girls - tomorrow. I'm not sure if any of them have met a real architect," Phoenix shared.

Stokely smiled as he mulled it over. Securing an opportunity to see Phoenix again warmed his hopes. He then answered and inquired, "Count me in. What time? Where? And what should I bring?"

Phoenix had assumed he'd require more convincing and was mildly surprised at his enthusiasm. But not only did she receive it, she made a mental note of it as well figuring if she were to be fair, she should make note of both positive and negative occurrences. Perhaps in time, one would outweigh the other.

"Cleage Academy - it's in the New Center Area on the service drive across the freeway from Ford Hospital." She waited a moment as recollection passed over Stokely's face. As it appeared that he could picture the school in his mind, she added, "It had been a closed Detroit Public School. But a community group who grew tired of lamenting what was wrong chose to do something proactive. The school has about 200 students and this is only its second year in existence. The administration partners with a handful of community organizations, BBD is one, to provide a real-life compliment to the curriculum."

She dipped a cheese covered chip into the salsa and scooped it into her mouth. She then continued, "The community centered approach is an extension of some of Reverend Cleage's community control ideas for schools."

Stokely chimed in, "Oh! The Shrine of the Black Madonna dude."

Phoenix laughed, "Yeah that dude!" She laughed, "That's who the school is named in honor of."

Stokely chased a piece of chicken around the bottom of the

plate with one of the last chips. Phoenix inserted jokingly, "You think you're going to get it?" To which Stokely responded, "Hunh?" Phoenix reached over, pinched the chicken with her fingers and rose to place it in Stokely's mouth. His eyes were surprised as he opened his mouth while smiling.

Phoenix resumed, "Our time with the girls begins at 10am. You don't need to bring anything, just be prepared to talk about your professional journey and answer a couple of questions."

Stokely gestured to Hannah for the bill and re-emphasized his intention to participate. While reviewing the receipt and reaching for cash in his pocket, he asked Phoenix, "Do you bowl?"

"Bowl?"

"Yeah, there's a bowling alley across the street. I mean you seem like cool people so I won't kick your butt too bad."

Phoenix laughed while replying sarcastically, "Oh, aren't you the gentleman."

CHAPTER THIRTEEN

LATER THURSDAY EVENING

Differentiating between snow or sleet is a futile exercise, regular folks just acknowledge the cold and do their best to get inside. Stokely and Phoenix were doing their best to cross Woodward Ave. arm-in-arm by braving the occasional stings on their faces from the frozen rain.

While stepping gingerly as if walking on eggshells with the hope of not breaking them, Stokely squeezed Phoenix's arm, smiled a sly smile, and said, "I've been here before." She blushed and went to slap him playfully on the shoulder as she said, "Oh, have you?" With childish instinct, he sought to move away from her slap while forgetting the black ice. In movements that mirrored an ice skater having a seizure, Stokely's arms and legs waved wildly prior to his behind coming to terms with Woodward's slick asphalt.

Phoenix covered her mouth with those mittens that have fingertips concealed underneath. The mitten portions flapped as she covered her mouth, clapped, laughed, and placed her hands on her knees before asking, "Are you ok?" A mid-80s

Buick Regal slid by with occupants pointing and laughing as the driver steered to avoid hitting Stokely and Phoenix. One of the teens inside the car yelled, "Get yo' punk ass up!" - Detroit hospitality, there's nothing like it.

Phoenix reached to help Stokely, but he waved off her hand to avoid pulling her down. After rising with one hand on his butt, looking like a pregnant woman attempting to support her lower back, Stokely meekly followed Phoenix across the street.

Once inside, after paying for a lane and renting shoes, Phoenix inquired again, "Are you going to be alright?" More embarrassed than injured, Stokely responded, "Beating you in bowling will help heal the pain." Phoenix smirked while slowly nodding her head up and down.

As they placed the house balls on the ball return machine, Stokely looked to Phoenix and said, "Can I ask you a very personal question?"

Phoenix answered with a reluctant and drawn out, "Ssuuurree."

Stokely, looking very earnest, said, "I'm really enjoying this time with you, except for crossing the street ..." They shared a laugh. "But I really need you to answer my question as honestly as possible."

Phoenix, uncertain of where this was headed said, "Ok, sure."

Stokely took a deep breath, glanced around the bowling alley, bit his lip, arched one eyebrow, crossed his arms, and asked, "What's the best Michael Jackson album?"

Phoenix couldn't control her laughter. "What?!"

"Nah, seriously. This is an urgent matter. What is the best Michael Jackson album?"

Still giggling, she answered, "Well, *Thriller* gets all the accolades and *Bad* and *Dangerous* were really cool. Plus, all jokes aside, I rather watch the *Remember the Time* video before

Thriller any day. But, in a very close race with my heart as a guide - I gotta go with *Off the Wall.*"

Stokely screamed "YES!!" as he jumped a few feet in the air and pumped his fist.

Phoenix couldn't stop laughing at his exuberance as she asked, "Why?"

Stokely looking like a mischievous child ready to tell a playground secret, answered, "My guys and I have this test - a litmus test. When spending time with someone you're interested in getting to know better, you gotta ask the Michael Jackson question."

Her laughter was nearing convulsive levels.

"Seriously, it tells the truth all the time. First, it sheds light on a woman's age or at least her maturity. So, if you're my age, the best answer is *Off the Wall.* If the lady responds *Thriller,* well you might have to ask a few more questions. But here's the deal, the *Off the Wall* lady is more of an independent thinker - she is her own woman. The *Thriller* lady may be young, tends to follow trends, or consumes music more so via radio or videos and less from listening to the whole album in one setting."

Still amused but intrigued that anyone would invest so much thought into such a pointless exercise, Phoenix nodded her head for Stokely to continue.

"Now if she answers *Bad,* that's bad. She probably is too young. Plus, everybody knows that if life was like the *Bad* video, you know like if Mike is in the subway and Wesley Snipes is about to jack him, Wes would kick his ass and then promptly avoid filing taxes on the loot."

Phoenix buckled over laughing as Stokely elaborated.

"For real though, now if the lady says *Dangerous?* You damn near in R. Kelly zone 'cause she is way too young." Then stopping to ponder how long ago *Dangerous* actually came out,

Stokely thoughtfully continued, "Well, I mean she may be of age but she doesn't know the real Mike."

Phoenix was amused and inquired, "What do you mean the 'real' Mike?"

Stokely was enraptured in the Michael Jackson theory and ignored her sarcasm while pressing forward, "The real Mike is the *Dancing Machine* Mike on the Gamble & Huff albums, right after being kid Mike with the Jackson Five. You know, when Jermaine left and they got Randy in the group. From *the Jacksons* album with *Good Times* and *Show You the Way to Go* on up through *Off the Wall* - that's the real Mike, our Mike"

"Our Mike? Oookkaayyy," she drew out the syllables in exaggeration while finding the conversation to be quite insightful to Stokely's heart.

Phoenix crossed one leg over the other, then with a nod stated, "Alright Professor, I have some questions of my own."

Stokely, still excited about Phoenix's correct answer, eagerly, "Yeah, go 'head."

"What about the young woman who chooses *Off the Wall*?"

Stokely was more than happy to respond, "She is hella cool. May have an old soul. Her parents raised her right. She probably has a good feel for history as well as our culture."

"Wow," Phoenix patronized, "This Michael Jackson test has all the answers."

After registering their names in the scoring machine, she stood up and reached for her ball. She turned with both hands awkwardly holding the ball, and with a very faint blush asked, "So you're interested in getting to know me better?" She let the question linger as she bowled a gutter ball. After which she complained aloud, "That always happens!" while throwing her arms up in feigned disappointment.

~

SHE WASN'T ALONE in disappointment. Tanya had returned to her hotel room and realized that not only did she not have a vase for the roses; she didn't have any shears to cut them down and had to use the ice bucket as a make-shift vase.

It hadn't yet been a handful of days, but she had already grown weary of takeout food. While takeout food was displeasing to her stomach, the serenity of being alone gradually increased her clarity with each slowly passing moment.

Recommitting to her marriage was her focus. Leaving Stokely in the past, a pleasant past but the past nevertheless, was an immediate course of action. More specifically, they needed to bring some type of resolution to their apartment lease.

That resolution would be an uncomfortable conversation. When they disagreed, Stokely chided her matriarchal ways. Having no children of her own, she resented his charges that she was being motherly. In time, she began to see that what he resented as her mothering more accurately reflected the gap between their ages.

What was perplexing to Tanya was not only did she not intend to have an affair; she never would have imagined falling so hard for a younger man. The decade plus between them was inconsequential when they were alone, but it was an impediment whenever they tried to plan ahead. In this regard, she was wrong. Stokely's reservations stemmed from the very omnipresent elephant in the room of their relationship, her marriage.

There would be no way around his mothering allegations when she shares that she has placed his half of the rent into a savings account. Oscar had paid the lease in full. The forms Stokely signed were never submitted and in their place, Tanya submitted paperwork identifying her as the sole leaser. She had no idea of how to breach the topic without some type of affront to Stokely's ego, so she left the matter alone. The matter caused her to sit on the edge of the bed and peer through the nighttime at the Detroit River.

There is no way she could pursue reconciliation with her husband with another man living in the apartment of which her husband had paid. Aborting the lease would cost her substantially; yet, she believed that allowing Stokely the weeks that remained in January was a suitable compromise toward concluding their affairs. Feeling assured that she was making the right steps toward preserving her marriage; she reached under her blouse behind her back and undid her bra. After pulling it through her sleeve, she flung the bra across the hotel room and lay back in bed with her roses.

BY THE SEVENTH FRAME, Stokely knew Phoenix had played him. Those first two gutter balls were ploys to fool him and he took the bait. While pontificating on the intricacies of the Michael Jackson test interspersed with excessive shit talking, Phoenix went on to bowl a strike, pick up two consecutive spares, bowl another strike, and finally a nine. The nine she bowled was a curler that hit the pin on one side and it ricocheted across the lane causing the other pin to totter but not fall. Stokely could only shake his head; he had only picked up one spare and bowled several seven and eight frames. There was no way he was going to beat Miss PBA Tour. To mock him further, she started singing Michael Jackson's *Got Me Working Day and Night* songs each time she bowled.

After wrapping up with a score well into the 200s, she did a 360 degree and went up on her tiptoes. She continued serenading or taunting Stokely, who bowled less than 80.

In addition to having busted his butt crossing Woodward, Stokely got his ass handed to him in a game over which he had talked so much trash. Yet, Phoenix's good natured taunting was full of smiles. To witness her smiling with genuine happiness was worth the ass-whupping.

As they turned in their rented shoes, Stokely asked, "Did you drive?" When Phoenix looked at him quizzically, he asked differently, "Can I get a ride? I left my truck on campus."

"Great, you have ice-chipping duty!" she responded. He assumed that meant yes.

This time as they crossed Woodward over to where Phoenix had parked in front of the restaurant, Stokely held her arm tighter both in jest and as a safety precaution.

"This would be your car," Stokely said with playful sarcasm. Phoenix drove a banana yellow Jeep Wrangler outfitted with 31-inch Mickey Thompson tires. She looked at him and said, "Just 'cause my baby yellow doesn't mean she's a cab. Anyway, with the butt whipping you suffered you might want to pipe it down a bit." She reached behind the driver seat to get the snow brush, tossed it Stokely, and hopped inside to start the engine. Stokely shook his head while thinking her spunk exceeded her size.

CHAPTER FOURTEEN

MUCH LATER THURSDAY EVENING

Her perfume was even more intoxicating in the proximity of her Jeep. With those super off-road tires, she made a slide-free U-turn on Woodward to head towards campus. Stokely looked out the window pondering how this last week of his life has been tumultuous. A week ago, everything was normal and then, what the fuck? But if it takes such a week to reach a moment like this, he'd undertake it again and again.

Phoenix stole glances at her passenger. His profile, the stubble on his face, and his repeated blowing into his hands and rubbing them together - what's that about?

"Do you want me to turn the heat up higher?"

"Hunh? ... oh, n'awl ... I'm fine."

"You keep blowing in your hands."

"My hands? Oh yeah ... I am. I'm not cold. I'm ... just thinking."

"You blow into your hands to think? You have to warm-up the gears of your mind or something?"

"You're funny. Make a right-on Warren. I'm in the parking structure across from the Science Center."

Silence returned to the Jeep as Phoenix made the turns that led her into the structure. They drove to the second level before Stokely pointed and said, "There we go."

He drove a dark blue Ford F150.

"Do you moonlight as a handyman or something? What's with the truck?" She really wanted to ask whether he had kids or a divorced wife somewhere, but managed to keep it civil.

"Well," Stokely replied after a deep sigh as he fished through his pockets for his keys. "I am an architect," his said with both his palms up and his shoulders hunched. "But really, I bought that truck so that I could haul materials. I used to own a home. I bought my house bare bones and sort of used my free time to renovate it to my taste."

"You used to own a house?"

"Yeah. Used to. The housing market crash that had everybody upside down on their mortgages hit me too. Around the same time, the firm I worked for folded because we had been squeezed out of some pretty promising contracts. Being an adjunct professor was supposed to be just extra money, petty cash that I used to fix up my house or you know, hang out in different cities."

He was more revelatory in the passenger seat than he had been all night. They idled behind his truck. Each statement he spoke sparked its own set of questions. While she really wanted to know, what took him to those 'different cities', she noted he hadn't mentioned a family.

"That's a lot of home repair to make you buy a truck," she said.

"Yeah, it is. Plus, my dad is a plumber, so every month or so, we kinda get together for old time's sake and tackle a small plumbing job." Stokely smiled at the thought. "My dad likes to explain plumbing step-by-step with me like I haven't been working with him since I was eight years old," Stokely laughed at the thought of his dad instructing him to make sure the pipes were secured in the bed of his truck. Or his dad's favorite adage which Stokely evoked for Phoenix using his father's Eddie LeVert voice, "Stokely, you know, first you gotta measure that pipe twice to make sure it's right before ya' cut it. Measure twice, cut once." Phoenix laughed while appreciating Stokely's nostalgia.

"We had totally redone my bathroom with one of those showers that you can sit down in and water sprays from various spouts in the wall. Real cool stuff ..." his words trailed off.

"Losing your house hurt you pretty bad, hunh?" she said in a consoling spirit.

"Yeah." He fumbled with his keys a moment before looking out the window and then resuming, "It's like the American Dream is a lie. You know all that bullshit we were programmed to think as kids about how owning a home was a great investment to build a financial nest. Bull. Shit. Trying to keep my house damn near pushed me to bankruptcy. The savings I managed to keep has been floating me the past year or so. But it fucks with me that my bank statements have withdrawals that nearly triple the number of deposits. I mean at this rate ..." he cut it short. If he kept talking, his living situation with Tanya would surface. He was convinced that going there would ruin the night.

He patted her hand as it rested on the stick shift, "Well, I won't bore you with all that. Maybe I can pick up with my story after I learn about you and Vallejo."

She smiled. She attempted to collect herself by switching back into professional mode. "Tomorrow, 10am at Cleage Academy - we're going to see you and learn about being an architect, right?"

However, her eyes said something else. Maybe an extension of what they were saying in the hall outside his office the other day. He didn't know. But he did allow himself the freedom to dive into the pool of her eyes and find comfort in their cocoa colored sweetness. After a few seconds, Phoenix smiled and then pointed at him while saying, "10 am now, I'm counting on you."

As he stepped down from the Jeep, he turned and said, "Phoenix, I'm there. I won't disappoint you."

Phoenix chose to not disregard the comment but didn't believe it either. Not because of anything Stokely had done, but more of a minimalist attempt to guard her heart. She placed his comment and what she believed was his intention, in her heart's purgatory.

CHAPTER FIFTEEN

FRIDAY MORNING

T anya sighed in disbelief, "Not another traffic jam." Last night's commute transformed from forty-five minutes into two and half hours. In a huff, she whipped out her smartphone to email the office.

She worked fluidly with her thumb while she held the phone in her right hand and mumbled under her breath, "I hate spell check."

A horn honking caused her to look up and see traffic had moved forward a bit. As she took her foot off the brake and gave the car a little gas, she noticed the semi-truck in front of her had Tennessee plates. The thought of Tennessee guided her thinking to Oscar, his roses, and Nashville. She smiled as she shifted her attention back to the email she was composing. She typed a message to the receptionist.

KAREN,

Traffic is bad. I may be running late for the debriefing session.

Tanya

THE MOMENT SHE HIT *SEND,* an unusual crunching sound caused her to look ahead in time to witness the Tennessee plate coming through her windshield.

"INNER CITY SCHOOLS," thought a slightly bothered Stokely as he searched the entranceway of steel doors for some type of buzzer. A voice crackled over the intercom, "Go to the door all the way down on the right, hit the buzzer, wait three seconds, and the door will open."

He searched for a camera to no avail as he tried to determine how the office staff even knew he was outside. The camera was as nondescript as the door buzzer. After a few seconds, he entered the school, and made a left turn into the main office.

"Good morning, how can I help you?" asked the secretary. An odd shaped woman with a pear head, multiple chins, and shoulders like coat hangers smiled at him with a cheerful disposition. Her pleasant spirit offset her awkward appearance. Stokely caught himself staring as if attempting to make sense of a distorted picture.

"Yes, I'm here to volunteer with BBD"

Before the secretary could respond, a voice came from around the corner near the staff mail cubby area, "Miss Gloria, don't worry I'll help him."

Stokely turned to face Regina.

She recognized him and extended her hand. "Hi, I'm Ms.

Dunbar. You must be the guest that Miss Ellison told me to keep an eye out for."

"She's sexy in school clothes, too?!" Stokely's thoughts raced as he searched her eyes for a clue of how he should play this unlikely reunion. She conveyed professional hospitality, so he followed along.

"Yes, Miss Ellison invited me. I'm Stokely Robeson."

They engaged in a two-pump handshake before Gina gestured to the binder on the countertop. "Mr. Robeson, we are so glad you are here!" She said excitedly. "If you could sign into the book, note the time - 9:56 - and then follow me. I'm hosting BBD in my classroom today."

Stokely really wanted to admire her beauty but he was too confounded with the notion that Gina and Phoenix knew each other. He signed his name as she spoke over her shoulder while opening the door, "Miss Gloria, I'll be back at lunchtime to order from your grandbaby's fundraiser."

"Hi, Ms. Dunbar," two girls waved as Gina and Stokely exited into the hallway. "Hey, Destinee and Jasmine!! How did y'all's dance recital go?"

Stokely was trying to be nonchalant but could not help but notice the tautness of the fabric straining to contain Gina's ass. "Damn!" he thought as the view conjured memories of the other night.

"Fine," the girls replied in a sing-songy childish choral response.

"That's good ladies. I'm going to need y'all to let me know in advance next time so I can come learn a step or two." The girls blushed as Gina continued "Girls, can you show Mr. Robeson to room 209 and let them know I'll be back in a minute?" It was more of a command than request. Gina placed a hand on Stokely's forearm while sharing, "Destiny and Jasmine will make sure you are there on time." Before he could respond, some other students had spoken to her and she began walking away with them.

Destinee had those horrible latches weave things in her hair. "Why would a parent do that to this adorable girl?" Stokely thought while wondering if there were grades of synthetic-ness because those things in Destiny's hair looked abnormally plastic-like. Jasmine seemed to bound when she walked, like a long jumper warming up before her event. Her buoyant strides cause Stokely to add a touch of joviality into his stride. By the time they reached room 209, the three of them were bounding down the hall like Laverne & Shirley in that show's opening montage.

Phoenix was in front of the classroom of nearly fifteen 11 to 14-year-old girls. As she spoke, she smiled at him and then glanced at the clock whose digital screen read 10:00.

She beckoned for him to come to the front, "Ladies, please allow me to introduce Professor Stokely Robeson. He is here this morning to share with you his story, particularly about becoming an architect." The young ladies offered a courteous round of applause.

As Stokely began to speak, Gina entered the room and headed toward the same set of seats in the rear of the classroom as Phoenix. "Damn, damn!" Stokely thought.

"Good morning, I'm Stokely Robeson..."

"Girl, who is he?" Gina asked Phoenix softly. "He is too fine!"

Phoenix blushed. "Professor Robeson is a contributor to the photo book I'm developing." Gina giggled "Phoenix, baby, that's bullshit." Phoenix playfully slapped Gina's thigh. Gina continued, "Girl, that book is still in the early just-a-step-away-from-an-idea stage. And this architect and professor believes in your book so much that he volunteered his Friday morning to talk to a bunch of girls he has no connection with ...." If Gina wore glasses, she would have been peering over the rims. Nevertheless, she looked at Phoenix with friendly incredulity.

Phoenix shifted uncomfortably. She reached to pat Gina's thigh but instead Gina caressed the top of her hand and squeezed it gently, "Phoenix, you're like little sister to me. Trust me, that man is interested in you. Don't overthink this." Phoenix turned to meet Gina's eyes but then looked to the floor. "Look when Elijah passed, my world was crushed. Part of my healing was accepting the temporariness of life. Moreover, I saw except for my grief that nearly all my worries and troubles were self-imposed. Once I accepted the necessity of changing that, I began to live more freely, more happily. Singing in the band? That's me trying to live more freely. Lord knows, my dating life has been sporadic, but when I do get together with someone - we have an amazing time." Phoenix was absorbing Gina's story like a sponge.

On the other hand, Stokely could not conceal his nervousness nor was he sure the girls were listening to him. They were so focused, it seemed insincere. "I earned a bachelor's degree in architectural engineering and my masters in civil engineering from North..."

Gina continued to hold Phoenix's hand while less than ten miles away, the emergency medical crew hoisted Tanya into the back of the ambulance. One of the emergency workers caressed Tanya's hand while repeating, "You're going to be just fine, just fine..." For Tanya, being late for work would be the least of her priorities once she regained consciousness.

CHAPTER SIXTEEN

___

LATE FRIDAY MORNING

"Why yo' school called A & T?" little Veronica inquired. Stokely thought she had been looking through him, but was happy that she retained something.

"It stands for 'Agricultural and Technical'. A few colleges used to have what they did as a part of their names. Maybe your grandparents attended a 'Normal School' ..." With that tangent, Stokely was sure he saw a few pairs of eyes gloss over.

"So, when do construction workers take over from the architect?" Tanesha asked.

"Great question! You have to realize that all things that are going to last, they got to go through a process. Like cooking a delicious meal or developing an important friendship." Three of the girls and Gina watched his eyes look to Phoenix when he said that 'developing' line. "So, the architect is at the very initial stages of the process and the construction workers are near the end. Some architectural firms include a construction arm, but those are the really big firms ..." More eyes glossed over.

Gina nudged Phoenix and used a husky voice to repeat,

"Developing an important friendship." Phoenix attempted to ignore Gina but the snicker that escaped her told Gina that she had heard her.

"Phoenix look here. I've listen to you complain about how the last few dates haven't worked out. If you fumble this one right here, I'm going to kick your ass." They laughed in unison while Stokely was beginning to sweat from nervousness.

"Is Miss Ellison yo' girlfriend?" Veronica asked. Stokely grimaced happily and if he could talk through telepathy, Veronica would have known he was asking her, "Why you gotta go there? I thought we were cool"

"Miss Ellison and I are collaborators on a book about some of the historic architecture around the city."

Starkesha, a fourteen-year-old girl who could easily pass for seventeen, smirked to one side of her mouth in disbelief. Regina stood and walked toward the door. Phoenix began gathering things as if she were going to resume leading the class. Thankfully, little Veronica got excited and turned everyone's attention away from Stokely when she asked, "Miss Ellison, you gotta a book? When can we read it?!"

Stokely exhaled and made another attempt at telepathy, "Whew, thanks for the bailout."

Phoenix returned to the front of the classroom while saying, "Ladies, let's tell Professor Robeson 'thank you' for sharing his story with us." Stokely waved good-bye while mouthing "You're welcome." As he exited the door to leave, he could hear Phoenix resume the BBD activity. Gina was waiting in the hallway.

"Thank you, Mr. Robeson," she said as she extended her hand to shake. Stokely shook her hand while searching her eyes for clues. She never blinked and her smile never wavered. Only time would tell, but he hoped that the things between them would remain unsaid.

AS HE MADE his way to his truck, he noticed several missed texts from the group chat between his guys.

Steve: It's on! Tonight - Flood's is the spot.

Wes: What time?

Terrence: It don't matter, it aint' jumping until I get there.

Steve: Man, please. Have yo' ass there by 9.

Wes: The wife goin' to let you out that late man?

Steve: Stokes? Where you at? Dawg, I'm grown, I get out when I want to.

Terrence: He probably playing housekeeper or trying to save some broad somewhere.

Wes: Captain Save 'Em!!

Terrence: I WANNA BE SAAAVED!!!

Steve: How many kids you got? Two? Aww, baby we goin' feed and clothe them kids.

Wes: Want to get yo cell phone turned on? I'll get it turned on in my name. Matter of fact, we can get that two for one deal down there at Cellular One.

Stokely: Fuck y'all.

Terrence: Captain is here!

Steve: Tanya let you join group chats now? She getting kinda lenient.

Wes: Y'all know that fool using the secret Metro PCS phone.

Terrence: The Bat Phone for the Captain.

Stokely: Man, what the hell?

Terrence: What the hell? Where you at right now? You either done saved or about to save some broads.

Stokely: In my truck.

Terrence: But where yo' truck at? You leaving the Save 'Em Anonymous Meeting?

Wes: Hi. I'm Stokely. And I be saving these broads.

Stokely: Man, I'm leaving a school.

Steve: Saving future broads? Or teaching saving tips?

Terrence: He is beating around the bush because he knows we right. Stokes, why you quiet? Tanya wit' you? You know participation in Save 'Em Anonymous requires sponsorship. Tanya still sponsoring you?

Stokely: I'll see y'all tonight. T, show up on time.

Wes: Bet, I'm there.

Steve: Cool, it's on.

Terrence: I WANNA BE SAVED!!! I'm there.

STOKELY SAT in the truck and expelled a long exhale. He hadn't told them that Tanya left. They like to fuck with him; but they wouldn't kick him while he's down. They often teased, "You the only fool I know that is content with being the other man." Whereas they could only hangout at designated times on the weekend because they were either married, soon-to-be, or serial monogamists, Stokely was the ever-available-on-the-weekend friend. Their wives and girlfriends were relentless is their efforts to play matchmaker for Stokely. That was Stokely's clue that his friends had not conveyed the nuisances of his relationship circumstances to their significant others.

He laughed a bit while thinking if he would've mentioned Phoenix or BBD that would have been fuel for the Captain Save 'Em fire. The fact that they could follow each other with jokes about a song that was over twenty years old is a testimony to their friendship and silliness. He was pretty sure he'd hear more Captain Save 'Em jokes tonight. Only thing that would change the subject would be if the eye-candy is on full tilt like it was on Wednesday. Or if Gina is performing - which he was sure he would not mention his experience with her to the fellas.

CHAPTER SEVENTEEN

FRIDAY EVENING

Gina's Groove was doing their thing when Stokely came through the door at 9:20. He stopped upon entering and shared a friendly smile with Gina. Gina winked in return while amid a soulful rendition of Earth, Wind, & Fire's *Reasons*.

Along with others around the stage area, Stokely sang along, *La La -LaLa -La La* until Terrence bumped him from behind and said, "Man c'mon with yo' falling in love ass." They dapped each other and headed to their spot in the back where Wes and Steve were already seated.

They sat there whenever they came to Flood's. While tonight it was an inconvenience because they really didn't have a view of the band, the location usually offered a healthy dose of eye candy as the ladies passed back and forth heading to the restroom. To someone eavesdropping on the fella's conversation, they could become perplexed at the number of pauses in the conversation. A typical conversation flows like this: "I'm just saying Chris Paul is that guy but I'd rather have ..." one of them would be explaining. Then another would do a head nod up and tilt toward the direction of observation. Two would follow the direction of the tilt while the other would attempt to surmise which direction the lady was headed so that he can begin looking in that direction in advance. Then as she entered his realm of vision, he would already be looking that way.

During the pause in conversation, each of them employs their own strategy for how they want to admire the approaching woman. Among them, they have come to respect each other's preferences - Steve is predisposed to large breasts, Terrence is tricky because the women he comments on are not the type of women he'd marry; but nevertheless, when he comments the lady is a sight to behold. Wes leans towards women of a lighter complexion - an endless source of ribbing from the others. Stokely favors the natural hair types of all complexions. Should the natural haired sister have full lips, Stokely undertakes some type of nonverbal action with an elongated sigh. He may stroke his facial hair, pull his earlobe, or take one finger and lightly scratch along his neck. To those other than the fellas, these are harmless, meaningless movements. But the fellas know, those movements mean an attractive woman is nearby so please be prepared for a visual delight.

After a pause of acknowledgement of the woman's attractiveness, their conversation resumes, ".... I'm just saying Rajon Rondo is my guy."

"Bullshit! Chris Paul the best point guard since Isaiah Thomas!"

"Hell nawl man, Isaiah ain't played in twenty years man; you just gonna skip over ..."

One of them would evoke Eddie Murphy in *Coming to America,* "Er'y time I bring up Isaiah Thomas some white person pulls Rocky Marciano out his ass."

Converse, pause, resume conversation, crack on each other, pause, joke, quote an old movie, and so on - that's the rhythm of their time at Flood's. A time none of them would say matters, but a time each of them looks forward to.

"Stokes!" Wes shouts.

"Yeah, I found this fool falling in love with ole girl singing with the band. Had to catch 'em before he put on his Save 'Em cape," Terrence injected while dapping Steve.

"She finer than frog hair though with them big assed legs," Steve said matter-of-factly.

"The band been up in here a minute, I'm sure she got a fan club," Wes added.

"Stokes' ass is the chairman," Terrence asserted.

A woman with tremendous breasts began heading to the bathroom. Stokely scratched his neck. Steve took a long drink from his beer as if the rim of the glass would camouflage his admiring eyes. Wes leaned back, laughed, and clapped as if viewing a comedian. Terrence hunched over and looked toward the bathroom door awaiting the lady to enter his line of vision.

"Aw shit man, she ain't got no ass," he confirmed.

Steve was more contemplative, "You know ass ain't everything."

The others looked at each other and burst out laughing. Steve, slightly embarrassed, took another drink.

"What's good with you man? The family alright?" Wes asked Steve.

"Yeah man, we 'bout to celebrate ten years of marriage," Steve replied.

"That's good shit dawg. I'm proud of y'all," Terrence added.

"Stokes, what's up with Tanya?" Wes asked.

The long pause made everybody look toward him. Steve had ordered him a Red Stripe in advance. Stokely reached to grab it for a sip.

"Damn. She left yo' ass?" Wes guessed.

"Shit, dawg. You homeless?" Terrence inquired sincerely.

97

"Nah man, she just ..." Stokely was reaching. "Man, I don't know what the hell just happened. But yeah, man, she dipped."

The elongated "DAAAAAAMMMMMNNNN" they would have said had to wait as a multi-colored haired woman strutted by. Each of their faces formed a variety of question marks.

"That's fucked up man," Steve answered. He then gestured to waitress to come over.

GINA'S GROOVE had begun a medley of DeBarge classics, they were in the middle of *Time Will Reveal* as the chorus filled the bar. It seemed as if the waitress walked along with the harmony. The fellas made no attempt to mask their appreciation for the curvaceous waitress as she sauntered over.

"Hey y'all back hunh? Y'all goin' to order some food or y'all just drinking tonight?" she asked. Considering how pretty she was, they all were going to order just to make her stand at the table longer.

"What's up with them jumbo shrimps?" Wes asked as if the shrimp would be different from the last time he ordered them. The waitress, being familiar with them, knew that his question meant he was ordering.

"Let me holla at the catfish, fried, with some of them greens and some mac & cheese," Stokely ordered.

Steve gestured to Terrence, who nodded. Steve then ordered, "Let's get a dozen of them chicken wings too." Then Steve went on while pointing at each of them, "Get this dude a Sprite, my man right here, grab him two of them Guinnesses cause his woman done left him, and this cat," he gestured to Wes with his thumb. "Get him some fruity shit with an umbrella on it."

They all laughed. "Nah, I'm kidding. Get this cat a Corona

but let him squeeze his own lime and shit 'cause he funny like that."

Stokely looked at his phone and saw a text from an unfamiliar number. He ignored it.

"Man, another year and the Lions ain't in the playoffs," Terrence mentioned.

"Man, them dudes ain't never trying to win. Just trying to sell tickets," Wes lamented. He continued, "Barry Sanders was right. They were trying to run him in the ground to sell tickets but they wasn't for real about no Super Bowl."

"Stokes, man, you gonna be ok?" Steve asked while Stokely was craning his neck for a view of Gina. She had just said that the band was going to take a break and would be back in a few minutes. Stokely was trying to see where she had gone.

"Stokes, Terrence called your ass right. Tanya gone and you done already fell in love with this singing chick," Steve summarized while reaching for his beer.

"Nah, I ain't in love ..." Stokely was saying before Terrence inserted, "Yet."

They laughed as Stokely continued, "But dawg, she's killing 'em tonight."

Then Wes pointed out, "Well get ready to die, because here she comes."

CHAPTER EIGHTEEN

LATE FRIDAY EVENING

She was conscious. Alone in a room at Hutzel Hospital, she felt thankful and stupid. Texting and driving accidents were things that happened to other people. She's too busy to have an accident over something so stupid. The doctors informed her that her injuries were minor due to the low speed of the car but they wanted to keep her overnight just to be sure.

Oscar was on stand-by for the last flight out of Nashville International. She was happy that he was coming. Maybe this was all a sign regarding the renewing of their marriage. Yet, she was troubled. Her texts to Stokely went unanswered. She wanted to resolve their business before Oscar arrived.

GINA DRAPED an arm over Stokely's shoulders. "Hey Stokely." She then looked to the guys and asked "Are y'all enjoying the music?" Terrence added "We enjoying the music and your legs!" They all laughed. With her left arm draped over his shoulder, she patted Stokely's chest with her right hand. "You really made an impression on our girls this morning. Thanks for visiting my class and working with BBD." She then looked to the others, "Y'all have a good time, alright?" Wes was smiling like the Cheshire Cat as they all watched her walk away. As she greeted another group of patrons, the fellas' looks turned to Stokely, who was ignoring the vibration of his phone.

"Aw hell nawl man," Steve said, "Don't be trying to act like ole girl just came over here on a whim. You already know her?"

"Stokes, you be keeping secrets, dawg," Wes added.

"What's with the classroom visits, man? I knew you was saving somebody!" Terrence exclaimed.

"Man, I ... Regina and me ... we ... we just cool that's all," Stokely said to satisfy their curiosity. It didn't work.

"Damn man! She put it on you too good. You're stuttering!" Wes exclaimed.

"Nawl, nah, no man," Stokely was getting exasperated as his phone vibrated again. "Dawg, let me take this." He unlocked his phone and began reading texts from the same number.

UNKNOWN: Stokely, it's me, Tanya. I'm texting from a new number. Call me.

Unknown: Stokely, please don't ignore my text. It's important.

Unknown: I've been in a car accident. Can you text me back please?

Unknown: I apologize for moving so abruptly. If you want to we can talk about that. There are some other things we should discuss.

Unknown: They are making me stay at Hutzel, room 615.

Unknown: Stokely please.

THE GUYS STARED at him as he read the texts. They could tell by his expression that he was troubled.

"Stokes? What you need man? What's wrong?" Steve intoned.

"It's Tanya. She's in the hospital. She says she needs to talk."

The waitress brought their food. They were so concerned for Stokely that they passed on the opportunity to bask in her smile or watch the sway of her hips as she walked away. Terrence swallowed a sarcastic quip he thought would lighten the mood. Steve and Wes alternated between watching the basketball game on the big TV, checking out the comings and goings into the ladies' room, eating, and watching Stokely. Any other night, he would have dove into the plate ferociously. Tonight, he was picking and nibbling.

Steve broke the silence. "Man, if she's in the hospital maybe you should go see her." The others nodded in agreement. Stokely looked as if it were a sudden stroke of genius. Terrence added, "Look you ain't gonna be cool until you know what's up. So, go handle that." Wes extended a fist pound which translated into 'Get going.'

Stokely looked at each of them nod their affirmation that he should leave. He stood, grabbed his coat, handed Steve a $20 dollar bill, and said, "I'll get at y'all. Thanks."

He was nearing the door as Gina was caressing the microphone. The band had already started with playing their next set. She could see he was bothered as she began singing DeBarge's *All This Love*.

Stokely lingered at the door a second longer. He was convinced that if there were no Phoenix, he and Gina could make it happen. But both Gina and Phoenix were ancillary matters right now, he needed to see Tanya.

CHAPTER NINETEEN

MUCH LATER FRIDAY EVENING

She was awake when he entered. While she had hoped he would come, she wasn't sure that he would. But the fact that he would come tipping in backwards after visiting hours was so like him.

As Stokely backed into the room and eased the door close, Tanya spooked him.

"Hi Stokely."

He was a little startled and found himself taking a deep breath before turning around. He had no idea what to expect but was committed to not allowing his facial expressions to trouble her. His preference was for the image of her sitting on the throne in their apartment to be the enduring image in the same way he wished that Michael Jordan's game winning shot in the NBA Finals over the Utah Jazz would be the enduring memory of him rather than those of Jordan in a Washington Wizards uniform. Stokely needed to accept that he was about to see her in a way that he hadn't before.

Stokely turned to face his friend, his lover, and the source of his heart's discontent. The bandage around her forehead was bulky but in an odd way appeared as a rim of a flower pot with her dreads blossoming above. The bandage and the nightgown contrasted with her beautiful ebony skin. She has a linen pants suit of a similar shade of off-white that when she wore it with the open toe bone colored heels - she could stop traffic in all directions. That's the Tanya he loved. This Tanya before him seemed weakened, still beautiful, but a silhouette of the woman he loved. Or maybe she was not the one who changed. Maybe that softening veil of love through which he viewed her had been torn. Now he was seeing her as she was and not who he dreamt her to be.

"Hey Tanya," he said meekly.

He pulled up the chair, took a seat, and reached to hold her hand. His eyes conveyed genuine care but his vocal chords were paralyzed with emotion. Tanya knew him well enough to know that his lack of words provided the best time for her share what she deemed as the necessities. She took a deep breath before she began. She patted his hand.

"Stokely. Stokely Medgar Robeson. I love you."

They both allowed her words to sink in. In hearing them, they recognized it as a first. He also saw it as the rose that would bear many thorns.

"I apologize for upsetting you. My sudden departure had nothing to do with how wonderful of a friend and lover you've been for me. It has everything to do with what I must do with my life. I wish my choices did not have to pain you." She paused for effect, then continued, "Choosing to have an abortion was my choice not an indictment of you or of us. It is not a choice that makes me happy or proud; it was just my choice."

Stokely wanted to reply. He wanted to question her abortion of their child and their love. She could see the questions burgeoning in his eyes but held up her hand to keep both his questions at bay and for allowance for the purging of her thoughts.

"Stokely, I do not want you to get angry with what I'm about to say."

With that statement, he could feel his anger beginning to simmer. The empathy for her, especially in her current state, mitigated that anger. His heart clenched in preparation for what was to come.

"I set up a savings account for you."

Stokely was confused.

Tanya continued, "The money you have been giving me for rent," she sighed. "I've been placing it in the savings account. I didn't have the heart to tell you the lease had been paid by my husband. I hope that saving the money and giving it back to you could be some sort of measure of peace between us." She waited for the questions that were passing through his mind like assorted ghosts flying throughout a haunted house. Finally, the assorted ghosts merged into one.

"So that's how he knew where we lived?"

Tanya's confusion showed through her expression.

Stokely continued, "The letter. The typed letter he slid under the door. He knew where we lived all along because he paid the lease?"

Recollection came clearly to Tanya. She typed the letter on an impulse. A terrible cover-up attempt that she knew she would regret.

She exhaled remorsefully. "Stokely, I wrote the letter."

The crystal vase in his heart that contained their love, slid to the floor, and shattered.

In seconds, his thoughts spanned an emotional continuum.

From pity to disappointment to hostility to appreciation, his eyes looked upon Tanya as if he never knew her at all.

She knew the door that led into his heart was closing. She made a last effort to stick her foot in the door's path by clutching Stokely's hand. She hurried the next statement. "Stokely, I terminated the lease. You have until the end of the month to vacate the apartment."

If impulses didn't have consequences or at least could be rewound and taken back, he would have unleashed a rage borne of confusion and feelings of being manipulated. But he stopped himself. Afraid of the type of violence he could do in his current state. He snatched his hand away from her and unconsciously wiped it on his pants leg. He found a spot on the floor to stare at as he made sense of the barrage of unwelcome news with which her 'closure' afflicted him. He could not shake the feeling of being played.

Tanya was both relieved and frightened. She watched as he stood slowly like an aging man. His fists were clenched at his side. As he reached for the door, he got a better idea. He turned and with an icy sarcastic tone said, "Mrs. Rousseau, what's my account number?"

Much like water spiraling down a drain, it was tangibly evident, that Stokely's feelings for Tanya were spiraling down an abyss. He was seething in disappointment. Yet, any show of anger would gain nothing. This was as close to a clean break as he could expect from a woman who wanted everything on her terms. He knew it would hurt, but there isn't a human defense mechanism that could brace one for these types of blows.

"I wasn't sure if we would talk again, so I mailed all the bank information to you this morning," she replied in a conciliatory spirit.

Stokely smirked. He then looked to the floor before glancing back up at her. He then said, "Or you could have slipped it under the door, I'm sure I would have gotten it." The "It" was pregnant with varied connotations. As he stepped into the hall, he looked back one last time. "Mrs. Rousseau, did your mother ever teach you that some things are better left unsaid?"

Without waiting for an answer, he closed the door to Tanya's hospital room and to her access to his heart.

CHAPTER TWENTY

AT THAT SAME TIME FRIDAY EVENING

To describe the flight to Detroit as a bumpy one would be an optimistic understatement. The keep-your-seat-belt-buckled light never dimmed. Three servings of Smirnoff and cranberry juice could not calm Oscar's nerves and the steady turbulence of the flight inflamed the precarious unsettledness of his soul.

He had no way of knowing Tanya's condition. After receiving a phone call in his office from the Michigan State Police, he was notified that she had been transported to Hutzel Hospital. Hours later, Tanya's text messages provided some assurance of her condition, but his fears wouldn't be placated until he saw her for himself.

According to weather reports, the torrential rain that tormented his flight probably would equal heavy snow for Detroit. As he peered out rain splattered windows, he thought about his commitment to make this marriage work. As a military man, he used his obligation to the U.S. Army as a facade to cover his inadequacies as a husband and a father. He had sent money and other provisions, but even by his own gracious calculations he had spent less than a quarter of his marriage in the same house as his family. They had learned to live without him. He moved on, but carried the failure of that union as his own self-inflicted scarlet letter. For his own sanity and sense of self-worth, his marriage to Tanya had to be different.

It just had to work. Throughout his life, he had been teased for being lucky. It wasn't his fault that his Creole family owned funeral homes in and around New Orleans for three generations. Nor was it his fault that in his first roll of the dice in investments, he purchased stock in a company that had only gone public some months before the end of 1980, simply because it was named after his favorite fruit. Nor was it his fault that his ex-wife was what many deemed as 'gracious' in their divorce settlement - she simply wished that they were apart - no child support or alimony. In his heart, those occurrences, while to his benefit, just happened and were not outcomes of his intentional action.

His marriage to Tanya was intentional, something he purposely set out to do and had succeeded in maintaining. Never mind that he was separated but still married when they met. Never mind that Tanya would not know 'abandonment' would be the rosiest way to describe how he left his wife and child. Never mind, that his mother gave an enthusiastic thumbs down of his choice of marrying another younger woman, this particular one she deemed 'too dark.' None of those things mattered. Not even Stokely mattered, who in a separate set of circumstances Oscar would have gladly mentored. There was not a thing that could come between him and making this marriage to Tanya work.

Eventually, Oscar's inner conversation dulled and he drifted off to sleep. He hadn't slept ten minutes before the plane made its beleaguered descent into Detroit's Metro Airport. Minutes later, he demonstrated reservation in opening the overhead carry-on cabin having feared that an avalanche would ensue as soon as he lifted. Instead, a passenger from across the aisle was besieged with luggage that had shifted during the flight when he opened the overhead bin. Somehow, Oscar managed to dodge trouble when it could be most damaging. Pulling his one piece of luggage, he made his way through the airport and to the car rental station at a pace that would have surprised his physician. He rented a Cadillac Escalade to handle the steady snowfall and proceeded with haste toward Hutzel Hospital. The aura of luck that followed him did not permit him to see the car that spun off the freeway on ice he had traversed just a minute earlier nor did luck allow him to recognize that the three cars that were pulled over by police between Telegraph Road and the Southfield Freeway were an exhaustion of the traffic cops on duty that night. Dashing through the snow in speeds that exceeded the speed limit, Oscar was both afraid for his wife and determined to make their marriage work.

CHAPTER TWENTY-ONE

SATURDAY MORNING

Saturday morning found Phoenix amid a weekend cleaning of her loft while singing along with the Michael Jackson playlist on Pandora. With a broomstick handle as a microphone and rhythmic shoulder hunches, she snapped her head toward the mirror and sang her version of *P.Y.T. (Pretty Young Thing)*.

Her choreography was a messy hodgepodge of steps from the *Billie Jean* and *Beat It* videos, but she was in good spirits as she danced and cleaned. She interspersed sweeping and leg kicks while doing her choppy moonwalk. She topped it with a 360 spin and an index finger point to the hallway mirror on cue with Mike as he sang about who he wanted to love and what type of love they needed.

Truly, she was enjoying her morning. After passing the Michael Jackson test, listening to his music made her feel closer to Stokely. As she spun swinging her hand as if it were on fire, her phone buzzed with an incoming email

SECONDS PASSED as Stokely stared at his phone wondering if he was pushing too hard too soon. With a deep sigh, he placed his phone down on the sink countertop, placed both hands on the counter's edge, and stared into the mirror studying his face while allowing his thoughts to drift into a medley of Michael Jackson's *Lady in My Life*. By the chorus, he was singing aloud and off-key.

By the time, he reached the part of the song about keeping the lady warm, his attention shifted to the steady snowfall outside his window. The snowflakes were as large and fluffy as cotton balls. By admiring the serenity, his spirit found solace with the snow.

WITH HER ARMS folded across her chest and phone in grasp, Phoenix leaned back onto the kitchen counter's edge and peered out of the window with a blushing satisfactory half smile on her face. As she followed the descent of snowflakes, she began to take inventory of her feelings and Stokely's email. There was no denying her attraction to him. Or was it admiration? Maybe both. Yet, that something between him and his ex-girlfriend gave her pause.

The email was a pleasant surprise. It was reassuring to know that as she was thinking of him, he was thinking of her. It was tempting to make more of the lines "I could really use a dose of your effervescent spirit" What does that mean? The email reeked of sadness. Almost as if he was reaching out for her from some dreary place. Then he asked her to join him OUTSIDE? Who does that? It's supposed to be work-related and he wants her perspective? He's the architect. Plus, who can be ready in an hour? Ninety minutes - maybe?

She replied to his email sharing her address and saying that she could be ready in 90 minutes.

One hundred minutes later, Stokely sat in his truck idling outside of Phoenix's loft. In the fifteen minutes that have passed since he arrived, he contemplated how transparent he should be about Tanya. He was in pain not because his relationship with her was over, but the way it ended. Every time he thought of the looming expiration of his apartment lease, he sneered. The attribute that bothered him most about Tanya was on full display last night. So concerned was she in making sure she dictated the conversation, they never discussed how she ended up in the hospital in the first place. Everything had to be as she planned, spontaneity be damned. What was more disconcerting was that there was no dialogue, just dictation. He would miss her, but he was starting to be glad it was over.

The knock on the window startled him. Phoenix was jittering up and down so he quickly unlocked the door. Once inside she emitted a "Brrrrrr" in reference to cold and snow outside. Stokely watched her. After she settled and smiled at him, he said, "Phoenix please do me another favor?" It was more of a formality than an earnest question. He turned off the engine and removed the keys. "Just for a second, I need you to stand back outside."

Hesitantly, she complied. Stokely got out also. He then ran around the front of this truck to the passenger side and opened the door. Phoenix acting on her initial offended feelings had begun to turn back towards her building. Curiosity caused her peek over her shoulder to see him run to her side. When she realized what he was doing, she blushed and climbed back inside. He closed the door gently behind her and made his way back to the driver side. After stomping the snow off his boots against the truck's running boards, he closed the door and started the engine. Phoenix smiled at him as he went reached to turn on the music. Using the iPod features on his phone, he generated a Norman Brown playlist. As Norman's guitar filled the cabin, Stokely got the truck in a slow crawl over scrunching snow towards Woodward Ave.

"Isn't it funny how the sky is so dreary and yet the snow is so peaceful, so calming?" Phoenix asked after they drove a few blocks. The irony that her synopsis of the weather matched his transitional feelings from Tanya towards her made him a tad reflective. A flicker of grief and hope passed his face like a shadow from a large airplane on a sunny day. Phoenix didn't know what to make of it but felt a tad more comforted when they reached a stoplight and he gave her a sorrowful smile. She guessed correctly that she was not the source of the sorrow.

He made a left turn onto Mack Avenue. "You're right about the weather. How it's both dreary and peaceful at the same time." Phoenix gathered that Stokely's eyes said he wanted to say more. What she did not know was if she would have to prime him or would he share at his own pace? The email, the invitation, and the fact that she was accompanying him, all alluded to some type of value he saw in her company. With that smidgen of hope, she promised herself that she would not over-think or judge too soon.

To the north, they could proceed along Dequindire Road. But Dequindire stopped at Mack and what should have been southbound Dequindire were train tracks heading towards the river. By utilizing the truck's 4x4 mode, Stokely hooked a right and drove down the snow-covered train tracks and gravel. After driving about 50 feet, he put the truck in park. To Phoenix, it appeared that he was squinting ahead. As a question moved from her mind and prepared to depart her tongue, Stokely inter-rupted by asking, "What do you see?"

"Snow?"

"Yeah, lots of that. What else?"

A bit confused, she answered, "Snow covered trash and debris."

"Too much of that," he responded matter-of-factly while nodding his head slowly up and down. Without taking his eyes off whatever he was staring at in the distance, he began explaining, "On Monday, I start a new job - a consultant job where I am expected to devise a renewal plan and design some renderings of how this train path could be a family friendly fitness walkway."

Phoenix looked out the front window again, while replying, "Oooohhhhh."

"Can you see that?"

She had turned her attention to him, as if by looking at his profile, she could 'see' how he thinks. She replied, "Not yet. You're gonna have to teach me." Like water seeping through soil, her words permeated his cloudy sky and gave birth to the brightest smile she had seen from him.

"I think I can do that," he said

CHAPTER TWENTY-TWO

SATURDAY MORNING

I t's odd to describe cottony-like snow as falling harder. Maybe it simply falls at a greater volume. Whichever it is, Stokely crept forward another seventy feet through the snow, then parked the truck, and hopped out. Reluctantly, Phoenix followed behind him. By this time, weather reports fluctuated between twenty or twenty-five inches of snow. Given they were traversing a desolate swath of the city; there were no tire tracks or previously worn paths. On another day, Stokely may have teased Phoenix about being vertically impaired, but today he kept it to himself while noticing Phoenix's high knee raises to get through the snow.

He reached for her hand and assisted her over towards him. He then instructed her to step into his footprints. With both hands behind him, Phoenix clasped them as if holding guide rails. They stopped about twenty feet from an overpass that appeared so decrepit that if drivers could see the support structures underneath, they would vehemently avoid driving over it. Yet, Stokely stood there marveling as if it were a newly unveiled

Augusta Savage sculpture. While he was consumed with his vision, Phoenix stepped close into his back. She drove her hands deep into his pockets and rubbed her nose against his coat at his spine. She then closed her eyes and nestled against his back as if he were her favorite pillow. One would be hard pressed to fit a credit card in the space separating her body from his. She was safe from the snow as he became enthralled with the possibilities of what could be.

They stood there for some time as Stokely made mental architectural analytics of the existing space. A casual observer would assume that Stokely stood alone.

The cold shiver that ran through Phoenix's body alerted Stokely that it was time to return to the truck. As he turned, he noticed that his footprints had been filled with fresh snow. He then bent low and told Phoenix to climb on his back. He scrunched through the snow like a climber carrying a survivor down Mt. Everest. He opened the passenger side and swung around so that Phoenix could slide easily into the seat. "She is so pretty," he thought as she got comfortable. He removed his gloves as he fished the keys from his pocket. Then he reached over her lap, inserted the key in the ignition, and started the engine. She quickly turned the heat on full blast as Stokely laughed. When she turned to face him, he used his thumb to wipe her nose. When she blushed, he noticed her faint freckles. The urge to view those freckles up close may have been his excuse, but the kiss they shared more than brightened her freckles and thawed their spirits.

"So, are you going to stand there all day?" Phoenix inquired jokingly.

"Uh no. You hungry?"

She nodded her head like toddler hoping for the last cookie.

As a precaution, due to the weather and the likelihood of trash buried beneath the snow, Stokely inched the truck back and forth several times before turning it around. He then crept along the what remained of the tracks he made earlier until reaching Mack. After turning left onto Mack, he asked, "What do you have a taste for?"

She shrugged. Stokely then asked, "You ever been to Mudgie's?"

"Nope, but I've heard about it. You want to try it?" she asked as if it were her suggestion all along. Stokely swallowed the impulse to be sarcastic and simply replied "Let's do it."

Stokely fought another urge. He was feeling some kind of way about Phoenix unplugging his phone and replacing it with hers. She searched through her playlist before arriving at Esperanza Spaulding. She watched as Stokely absorbed Esperanza's string harmony. She smiled as he began to nod his head. "You aren't the only music fan around here!" she announced. They both laughed as Stokely sloshed through the snow.

CHAPTER TWENTY-THREE

SATURDAY AFTERNOON

"If you would have told me upfront that we were ordering grilled cheese sandwiches and bowls of tomato soup, I would have passed. But dang Stokely, lunch was really good!" Phoenix shared as she extended an open palm to high-five Stokely.

"It really did hit the spot," he replied. He smiled knowing that she enjoyed the food. He also noticed that within himself, he had never been here. He was what those Zen guys call "In the moment." She was happy. He was happy and they were enjoying each other's company. It was so different from Tanya, who was so consumed with what was supposed to happen next that he recognized that he had developed a habit of looking ahead as opposed being present in the moment.

Phoenix looked out the storefront window next to where they were sat, "Doesn't look like it's going to slow down does it?"

"I wouldn't want you to," Stokely's thoughts snuck into his response.

Phoenix's brow furrowed as she attempted to contain a

smile. She looked at him quizzically, cocked her head to one side, and said, "Whatcha talkin' 'bout Willis?"

They burst into laughter and startled the waitress who was approaching with their hot tea.

Stokely apologized to the waitress before turning to Phoenix, "I meant to say - yeah, this snow just keeps on falling." His schoolboy smile did not satisfy Phoenix's raised eyebrow. He tried again, "I'm enjoying this time with you and ..." he began blushing as he looked down at the table, "... and I just really don't want it to end."

Phoenix smiled harder before sipping her tea. "I'm enjoying hanging with you too."

In an attempt to change the conversation, Stokely said, "When we met you said that your interest in the buildings and being from Vallejo and here - you said that was a long story." He looked out the window and did a gesture with his palm raised like Vanna White highlighting a prize on The Wheel of Fortune, "It looks like we might have time." The schoolboy smile worked this time.

With a straight face, Phoenix looked at him and rapped the hook from Ahmad's *Back in The Days*. Prompting them to laugh once more. Stokely followed with "Phoenix, you are a clown!" To which she replied, "Ok, seriously though." She was working to catch her breath from laughing. "I was raised in Vallejo. I guess for you, it would be like Inkster is to Detroit - that might be one way of looking at Vallejo in comparison to Oakland. Working folks, most of whom migrated from Louisiana, Texas and other parts of the South." She took another sip of her tea.

"My Nana graduated from Grambling and moved to California with my grandfather, W.J. That's his name, W.J. Like he had so many siblings they ran out of names and just started using abbreviations." Stokely smiled knowingly as if he understood that naming practice. He then inserted, "Almost like them old cats named General or Mister." Phoenix laughed along, "Right, right, but don't get that confused with Priest. If you're named Priest, that means yo' mama had a thing for Superfly!" They couldn't stop laughing.

"Alright, alright. My Papa and Nana moved to Vallejo in the 50s. Nana kept house while Papa became a longshoreman. According to my mother, Nana loved Papa but hated the domestic arrangement. Papa had some down-home notions about a woman's place. Most people view folks who participated in the Great Migration as a people fleeing racism and looking for jobs. Nana was kinda ahead of the curve, she wanted to go somewhere where a woman could be a woman. Going to California was her idea. If it were left to Papa, they'd probably would've stayed in Louisiana."

Stokely was paying full attention. Assured that he found her history lesson worthwhile, Phoenix continued after another sip of tea.

"My mom was born in 1961 and that somewhat quelled Nana's complaints about domesticity. But isn't funny how life can throw some curveballs? Papa was what they called a 'man's man'. Stocky, gruff, hard-working and then some but then you got little Nana - me and Nana are the same height and dress size. My mom is the tallest, she's five foot two," Phoenix giggled. "But little Nana could keep Papa grounded. Then around the time my mom was eight, everything changed."

Stokely listened intently, even leaning forward after taking a gulp of tea.

"Papa was at some type of union gathering that turned ugly. There was a scuffle with the OPD and Papa took a bullet to the head."

Stokely gasped.

"He lived; but then to hear Nana tell it, he wasn't never the same. Nowadays, you could have a big lawsuit or something.

But then ..." Phoenix drew an arc with her index finger as a non-verbal cue distinguishing a time distant from the present. "...back then, folks had to be happy to be alive. The incident gathered the attention and support of the Panthers but Nana was just kinda in a daze you know." Phoenix cast a reflective gave toward the falling snow.

A pleasant thought caused her to smile as she described, "Nana's baby sister, Gladys, left Bishop College to move in with Nana, my mom, and Papa. You know how people say during funerals and stuff," Phoenix changed the pitch in her voice, "if you need anything just call?" Stokely smirked and nodded in agreement. "Well, I don't think Nana even called. Gladys got the news, dropped her life in Dallas, and moved to Vallejo."

Phoenix continued, "My mom says she got her sense of style from Aunt Gladys. Imagine being a little girl having your 19 or 20-year-old aunt living with you and your mother. It's almost like a heaven sent big sister or something. Anyway, I'm not sure if Gladys had been there a year before Papa died. But Nana feels that he really died the day of the shooting. Because the Papa she loved would have never wanted to be totally dependent on a woman in the way he was during the last months of his life. If you asked Nana today, she would describe those months after the shooting as a prolonged grieving period. By the time a blood clot led to a stroke, Nana felt robbed of the life she knew but oddly able to work toward a life she wanted. By the next school year, she was teaching elementary school."

Stokely was enthralled and warmed by the image he conjured of Phoenix's family.

"So, my mom grew up in a house with her mother and aunt. Obviously, Gladys is younger than Nana and she was impressed by the Panthers. Nana wasn't. You know people assume all the Black people in the Bay loved the Panthers, but it wasn't like that. Some did and they were supportive and all that. But there were some who weren't. Nevertheless nowadays, we get caught up in picking sides, but why does it have to be that way? Gladys wanted to do something for the people, so she chose to work with the Panthers. But Nana? She served the people through the classroom while staying away from the Panthers. Primarily, she avoided the Panthers because she thought Eldridge Cleaver was full of shit."

Stokely was surprised but laughing as Phoenix elaborated, "Nana says it isn't ladylike to curse. But when it comes to Eldridge, she calls him a 'shit-starter' in a heartbeat. She never talks bad about Huey or Bobby. She reserves her disdain for Eldridge. She calls Elridge's book, *Soul on Ice* - garbage. My mom says the way Eldridge talks about women and rape in the book put him on Nana's permanent despised list."

Stokely shook his head as if saying, "I can believe it."

"Soooooooo," exhaling a drawn-out sigh, Phoenix continued, "My mom is spending hella time with Aunt Gladys who admires the Panthers. While I don't know who little Black girls in the late 60s and early 70s idolized, my mom idolized Elaine Brown and Ericka Huggins."

Stokely looked a little confused.

"I'm glad my mom isn't here. She'd kick your ass if you didn't know who Elaine and Ericka were." Phoenix said while folding her arms across her chest.

"Elaine and Ericka were leaders in the Black Panther Party. Well, more so Elaine, but Aunt Gladys just thought the world of how Ericka balanced her commitment to the movement as a single mom whose husband had been murdered. With Aunt Gladys, both Elaine and Ericka are held in high regard. My mom loves to talk about when she met Elaine who was running for city council or something. Mom makes it seems like she worked on Elaine's campaign, but she probably only passed out a few flyers. But I imagine if you're eleven and you meet the lady your Aunt hails as a hero and that lady is running for a political office... well, you'd be quite impressed too. My mom swears Elaine told her 'Power to the people little sister' when she was campaigning one day. Phoenix chuckled, "Whatever Elaine said, she certainly cemented herself as a lifelong hero for my mom."

The afternoon sky was just beginning to darken and there weren't many patrons in Mudgie's. Stokely asked "Would you want to split a Fudgie Mudgie desert?" Phoenix answered, "Yeah that'll be cool." She then asked, "Am I boring you? I mean all this history and family stuff, you're really interested?"

Stokely eagerly replied, "Yes. Understanding you is easier now that I know your story."

Stokely extended his fingers one at a time as he named bits from her story. "Grandma's spunk or determination. Elaine and Ericka. Serving the people. Your height? It all kinda comes together now." Phoenix gave a playful glare when he referred to her height but then resumed her story.

"I guess the big part of my story is that the women in my life, they all had this aspiration to experience life beyond their environment. First, Nana left Louisiana. Gladys moved to Dallas and then Vallejo. My mom went back to Louisiana, for school, and then after raising me in Vallejo, up and moved to Detroit." Phoenix's restated it with emphasis, "Detroit? I mean who says, you know what, fuck it, I'm moving to Detroit." They both laughed.

"I did."

"Yeah, but you're from here. You mean when you graduated?"

"Nah, my first job was in D.C. I lived there for a couple of years."

"D.C.? Well, that explains all the walking."

Stokely was a little puzzled. Phoenix leaned across the table, gently touched Stokely's hand, and whispered, "Stokely honey? What Detroiter you know walks as many places as you?"

He laughed. She was right. He enjoyed walking and in D.C. he walked nearly everywhere. His car collected more dust than miles.

CHAPTER TWENTY-FOUR

LATE SATURDAY AFTERNOON

Dessert arrived. Stokely and Phoenix exchanged mischievous smiles. He gestured for her to take the first bite. She sank her fork in the corner teasingly before scooping a small section. Cupping her opposite hand under the fork as she raised it to her mouth, she took a bite. Her eyes rolled back into her head as she hummed "Mmmmmmmmmm." She then used the fork to point to the brownie and while still chewing attempted to say, "This is good."

With a mouth full of fudge, her words were mumbled. Stokely then mocked her back saying "Mis mis moood."

"Shut up Stokely!" she blurted playfully as she finished chewing. "You better get some before I finish it." He took a bite and nodded knowingly. It was good.

"Tell me more about you, about D.C."

"Nah. Unt-unh. I mean I will. But you ain't finished yet," Stokely retorted. "I mean, I'm seeing this little pretty girl with an afro, probably about your height ..."

Phoenix raised a fist as if indicating she was going to punch him. Yet, the brownie was holding her back.

"... this little pretty thing meets Elaine and then you're here today? Nah sister, go on and finish your story."

Phoenix smile and resumed, "My mom met my dad at Grambling. He was like a super-duper senior or something he had been on campus so long. Nana never liked him. She called him 'Smokey' after Smokey Robinson and in reference to his light complexion. It was regarding my father that she created this Nana-ism ..."

Phoenix sat upright to change the pitch of her voice, shook her right index finger, and placed her left hand on her hip, "Baby don't ever date no man prettier than you!"

Stokely wanted to laugh but clearly needed an explanation. Phoenix obliged, "Nana says that pretty men are too much hassle. Handsome is better. Ruggedly handsome like Papa is best. But a pretty guy, Nana despises them just a little less than Eldridge Cleaver." They laughed while working their respective ends of the brownie. Phoenix went on, "I'm not sure if my father considered himself as pretty but he sure had my mom gone. My parents were married for the first six years of my life or I should say fourteen, but I last saw my dad when I was six. They were separated for years before divorcing. While I know my mom got an awesome job opportunity that led her to Detroit; now that I'm older, I'm convinced she may have also hoped for one last chance with my father."

Phoenix cast a faraway look out the window while explaining, "If I didn't know my mom, I'd probably have all kind of misperceptions about her ambitions for a relationship with my father. Yet, being there, close up? She always carried herself with strength. She never cast aspersions about my father. She would simply say, 'Honey, don't waste your time trying make a man be where his heart isn't.'"

To demonstrate how much he was listening but also to steer the conversation away from what seemed to be an uncomfortable topic, Stokely said, "So the travel-far-away-from-home-to-define-myself gene in your family shows up when you go to Bennett?"

Phoenix nodded appreciatively toward Stokely while stating, "Yeah, us Ellison women we got to get up and go when the spirit hits us." Her laugh was faint. She was glad that Stokely had steered the conversation away from her dad. Inside, she kicked herself for still having not called her father after finally convincing her mother to give her his number.

"I hope the spirit doesn't hit you anytime soon," Stokely said slyly.

His statement drew Phoenix out the of the vertigo of worry that overtakes her when she thinks of her father. Stokely and his flirtatious comment were a lifeline at that moment. A lifeline that she appreciated. She looked him directly in the eye and said, "The spirit hasn't moved in me for a while. Until this week, I was wondering where it had gone." Phoenix could be flirtatious too.

Stokely signaled for the waitress. He was reaching for his wallet when Phoenix waved, 'no.' She reached in her purse while stating, "Allow me. Today has been therapeutic and ... well, I've enjoyed your company, too. Please allow me." She placed twenty-five dollars on the table and began to pull on her coat.

As Stokely stood and began zipping his coat, he asked, "You mind going for a ride?"

"You just don't want to take me home do you?"

Stokely blushed, "Nah, not really."

Phoenix laughed, "You want to drive in this snow?"

"With you? Hell yeah!" he said as they moved to the door.

There Stokely squatted as if motioning for her to get on his back. She hopped up as he commenced to trudge through what appeared to be twenty something inches of snow.

CHAPTER TWENTY-FIVE

LATER SATURDAY AFTERNOON

"The car suffered more damage than she did," thought Oscar. He took a seat on edge of the hotel bed while placing her things on the floor between his legs. Tanya came in and went straight towards the bathroom. Oscar began recollecting the last twenty hours or so - heading to the office in a heartbroken slump, the phone call from the police, the phone call to his travel agent, the hurried packing, the tumultuous flight, the snow, seeing his wife bandaged in the hospital bed peacefully asleep. He sat in the chair next to her bed and wondered why it had been angled toward the bed instead of being flush against the wall. Once he scooted the chair back to the wall, fatigue overwhelmed him and snores began to escape him.

Just like in the hospital earlier that day, Tanya nudged him awake. Just like in the hospital, his heart warmed exponentially to awaken to her beauty. Whereas in the hospital, her nudge was playful, in the hotel, her nudge led to a caressing of his thigh. Tanya placed one knee on the edge of the mattress and moved into a crawl along Oscar's body. He smiled as she nuzzled her nose near his belly button, again at his diaphragm, and then kissed him lightly on the chin.

Right then, in his mind and his heart, Oscar pledged to discard the every other Saturday regimented approach to love-making. Tanya emitted a low "Mmmmmm" as she could feel his erection pressing against her thigh. She ran her cheek along the stubble on his jaw line, licked his earlobe, and said, "Oscar, I want us to work." She then drew a line with the tip of her tongue along the rim of his ear. He patted her ass with both hands, as if sending a tribal drumming message that said, "I do too."

She began to grind against him while playfully kiss-pecking his lips. Even in foreplay, Tanya likes to be in control and at this moment, Oscar was more than happy to oblige.

"NO SUGGESTIVE MUSIC FOR THE RIDE?" Phoenix joked.

Stokely smiled but was focused on keeping both hands on the steering wheel. Even with his truck in 4x4 mode, driving was perilous. As he made a left off Rosa Parks onto Michigan Ave, he mentioned "Remember walking down this street?"

In sarcastic jest, Phoenix responded, "No, I only remember narrowly missing the punch that sent my former colleague sprawling across the pavement."

Stokely attempted to watch the road and search her face for clues. He proceeded down the avenue at about twenty miles per hour. Traffic was sporadic and the sun was making its descent into the horizon.

He hung a right onto West Grand Boulevard and began to warm up his version of a long story.

"When I saw you the other night, at Slow's, the lady I sat with was my, my, um, she was my ex."

She turned to face him. "Stokely, why do you stutter when you talk about her? Are you still in love with her?"

He took a deep breath. "Well, I don't believe that if love is genuine, we can fall in and out of love with someone. Tanya is in the past. I accept that and it's cool. It's what I want, what we wanted, you know?" He looked to Phoenix. She didn't flinch or otherwise respond.

"I stutter not about her or lingering feelings about me and her." At the light at West Grand Boulevard and Warren Avenue, he took a deep breath. "I stutter because she was married, we were living together, and I didn't want you to think less of me because of that." Phoenix could hear Stokely's long exhale. She sensed, correctly, that this was a pivotal moment in their friendship. As he proceeded through the intersection, Phoenix assured him, "Stokely, I won't think less of you for having lived with a woman you care about. I'll only think less of you if you aren't forthright about it being over with her."

Stokely nodded slowly at first and then a bit more enthusiastically as he turned to her.

"Bet. Forthright is easy."

They nodded at each other as the boulevard bent in an eastern direction while going over I-96. Phoenix's nod meant "I'm glad you are agreeing to be forthright." Stokely's nod meant "She's even cooler than I thought."

He resumed, "It was just a few days ago, but when I came home, all of Tanya's belongings had been moved out of the apartment. Furniture, most of it, clothes, make-up, mail, picture frames - everything. Well, except for a reminder to call LaDonna who took care of her dreads."

"Hey, LaDonna hooked up my twists!" Phoenix exclaimed, interrupting Stokely's thoughts. Stokely removed his hat and ran his fingers over his close-cropped haircut and added, "Looks like I got sometime before I make my appointment with LaDonna, hunh?"

They both laughed before he returned to his thoughts about Tanya's departure. He sort of spoke and sort of questioned aloud, "It had to be professional movers."

He paused a moment before continuing.

"The assumption is professional movers means that it was planned. As far as I know though, there were no signs. I mean in retrospect, when you're in a relationship with a married person, it's only so far the relationship can go, you know?"

Phoenix inserted, "I do not know. But it makes sense."

Stokely was a little tentative as to whether he was going too far but he also appreciated the soothing effects of being able to verbalize the circumstances. He continued.

"It's like being in a perpetual holding pattern." He paused while accepting a truth he had been ignoring all along. "I guess it doesn't matter if there is no other reason to break the holding pattern. People get comfortable. They know it can't last, but they kinda enjoy, relate, maybe even love each other in the meantime." By now he was speaking more to himself than Phoenix but she watched a gradual ease come over him the more he talked so she didn't interrupt.

"There's your building," he pointed out in reference to the building captured in Jake's photographs. Phoenix nodded in agreement without losing her listening posture.

"To be honest," Stokely continued, "I suppose the pain is in the abruptness of her departure as opposed to the fact that it's over."

"Would you have preferred that she strung out the inevitable?"

The corners of Stokely's mouth turned down and his lips pressed together as if pondering the stringing out notion heavily.

"Nah, stringing it out would be worse. I guess abrupt is better."

Phoenix added "Stringing it out could be torture, but what you call abrupt sounds more like an act of certainty from a grown woman."

More so in an act to extend time with Phoenix than anything else, Stokely made a left on Rosa Parks Boulevard, a street the old heads called 12th Street. He did so while digesting Phoenix's last statement. It was as if a light switch was turned on in his mind. "Tanya does not have to be a bad person," he thought. "Hell, they had too many good times for him to even try to go there. She simply chose to act on a personal choice, just like Phoenix said."

Phoenix could sense the that conversation had run its course. She looked out the window and said, "Some of these buildings are still burned out from the riot."

"Rebellion," Stokely said in a correcting tone.

Phoenix turned to face him with a look of uncertainty.

"A riot is something that is out of control, no focus, no target. They call it riot. We call it the Great Rebellion or an insurrection. It had a target and a purpose. We can't let them define our actions with misleading terminology."

"OOOOkay Dr. John Henrik Clarke," Phoenix responded jokingly. Stokely laughed a bit with her. He went on, "You talked about your mom and great aunt and their interactions with The Black Panther Party. My dad worked with The League of Revolutionary Black Workers.

Phoenix had never heard of them. She turned her body to him attentively.

"It's like this. When is the last time you read about some San Bushmen in the Bible? Never, right? But that doesn't mean that their culture did not exist. The absence of their story in that particular forum doesn't equal non-existence."

Phoenix began to feel her John Henrik Clarke comment may have been more fitting than she initially thought.

Stokely continued, "We hear about the Civil Rights Movement and the Black Power Movement but way too often the accounts lend themselves to an assumption that those were the only organized movements of Black folks trying to take greater control of their destiny." Stokely could feel himself getting on a roll. He took a deep breath and shifted the gears of the conversation. "I don't want to preach Black History to you." He paused smiling.

"Honestly, I just don't want to take you home. Like I said earlier, I don't want today to end."

"That's nice Stokely. I feel the same way. But since we're being honest, I have to use the bathroom. Can you turn this truck towards Midtown and step on it a bit?" They laughed.

"How about you coming to church with me tomorrow? You could meet my mother."

Stokely hung a right onto Clairmount and made his way over the Lodge Freeway service drive. His smile brightened as he contemplated meeting Phoenix's mom.

"Cool, what time should I pick you up?"

Phoenix was relieved that he didn't leave her hanging. She started a statement and stopped, "I'll text you," she paused. "We don't have each other's number!" They laughed some more.

"Give me your phone."

Stokely's heart skipped four beats.

"Boy give me the damn phone, I ain't going to scroll through the pictures of your ratchet cousins!" They were hysterical with giggles as Stokely handed her the phone.

"Rise. That's my password. R-I-S-E."

Phoenix unlocked the phone and commenced to saving her number in the address book.

"I'll message you a picture tonight for you to save with my number."

Stokely's heart surged with joy.

CHAPTER TWENTY-SIX

SATURDAY EVENING

There aren't many things that bring greater peace to a troubled man's soul than the deep sleep that follows great sex. Oscar was proof of that fact as he had fallen into a Mariana Trench-like deep sleep. He hadn't rolled over. He hadn't pulled up the cover. He was like the old Richard Pryor joke: he came and went at the same time.

Even though it was Saturday, Tanya was assured that this was the start of something new. She chuckled as she thought about how Oscar stood up in it with more rigidity than before. She considered for the first time whether she had some accountability in the bland sex life they shared. She was receiving a steady sexual diet from Stokely and giving Oscar the reheated leftovers. When she served Oscar the main dish, like she did this afternoon, he met it with a grand appetite. The thoughts reminded her that the success of their marriage was a responsibility to be equally shared, not any one person's fault.

She kissed Oscar's forehead lightly as she rose from the bed. A peeping tom would have been overflowing with delight to see such a beautiful woman standing naked in the window. But unless that peeping tom had a super-powered telescope that can zoom across the Detroit River from Canada, there was little chance of anyone seeing her as she stood in a window on the sixty-seventh floor.

As she tilted her head to the left, Tanya could catch a slight view of Fort Street. A small smile crossed her face as she reflected on a childhood spent catching the city bus with her mother up and down Fort Street.

She had been raised in house on Frazier near Coolidge in River Rouge, a small south western industrial suburb of Detroit. Her grandfather built the house for his family but by the time Tanya was seven, only her and her mother considered it home. Her grandfather had died of lung cancer after decades of a pack-a-day cigarette habit. Days later, her grandmother passed from what Tanya's mother called a broken heart. Technically, Tanya's drug addicted uncle was still alive but after decades of abusing drugs, his yellowed, monstrous looking face was the best attribute of his drug infested, needle mark riddled body. Once during her junior year at Southwestern high school, Tanya was awakened to the loud crash of broken glass. Her uncle was attempting to borrow some of grandmother's precious China dinnerware. As he turned to depart, Tanya's mother was cocking a snub-nose 38 Special right at the tip of his nose. They haven't seen or heard from him since.

There it was, Fort Street, running southward in the bottom corner of view from the hotel. She could see the Ambassador Bridge where her mother worked as toll both operator for twenty-seven years. They never owned a car which fueled Tanya's passion for cars. After earning a scholarship to Central State University, the memories of those bus rides along Fort and the life lessons taught by her mother pushed Tanya toward engineering and graduate school. Now, here she was, years later, looking down on the one street that was a unifying thread in the fabric of her life.

The sun was starting to set when she walked over to the desk with the thought of ordering room service. She glanced over at Oscar. The way he was laying across the bed, she was sure that he was enveloped within the sweetest of dreams.

AFTER CARRYING Phoenix to the doorway and sharing a goodbye kiss, Stokely made a promise to himself to do things differently. Unlike too many of his previous dating experiences, this time the pursuit of sex would be diminished. This time was going to be different because he will be different. He was choosing to match his 'feelings never felt before' regarding Phoenix with 'dating-behaviors-never-tried-before.' The evidence of that was his willingness to share his phone and pass-word, agreement to meet her mother, and go to church. Church?! He was certainly doing things differently. He swung a left off of Canfield onto Woodward and began heading to South-field to visit Steve's house. He knew Steve and Wes would be watching the Pistons. Talking about whether the Pistons hired the right coach would keep his mind off of the loneliness that awaited him in his apartment.

OSCAR AROSE to the inviting smell of crab cake sandwiches and a talkative Tanya. She poured him a glass of sweet tea and then placed his sandwich plate on the bed. Oscar couldn't find his underwear and proceeded to don his slacks commando style. The way she sat on the edge of her seat alerted Oscar that she had plenty to say. He pulled his t-shirt over his head, mouthed "Thank-you" towards Tanya, sat, and reached for his plate. She allowed him a moment for grace before proceeding.

"I put a deposit on the cutest little townhouse the other day. We should go see it tomorrow. It's already modestly furnished so I only have to add my special touch to make it feel a little like home." Indirectly, she was informing Oscar that she had moved out the apartment she shared with Stokely while also affirming her desire to continue with her job.

"When do you plan on moving in?"

"Tomorrow if you feel like it. I have the keys already. Let's drive out and look at it in the morning. It's not far from Big Beaver Road in Troy. Remember where the Delphi headquarters was?" Before he could answer, she responded, "It's not far from there."

The elephant in the room was Stokely. If Oscar allowed himself to think about it, his thoughts would surmise that Stokely visited her in the hospital. He felt he had a pretty good handle on his wife. She tended to be talkative about topics of her choice, but if the topic was uncomfortable she would not discuss it. Instead she'd write a note. Oscar wanted to be safe in his assumption that if she has a new place, she must have dissolved the lease of the apartment she shared with Stokely. His wife's other man living in a place he paid for was a revolting thought. Plus, while he was managing a shred of composure about her affair, he knew it would be totally out of character for her to let Stokely live rent-free.

"Would the commute would be much better than your last place?" Oscar asked in a veiled reach for information. Tanya heard and dodged it.

"Much better. I could even go back for lunch, eat, return to the office, and still not miss a beat," she said with a little extra charm.

"They didn't give you a hassle about breaking the lease downtown, did they?"

Tanya rolled her eyes in an act to feign exasperation for the managerial staff, "They have a quandary of fees if the place isn't rented. But I know they have a waiting list. I would not be surprised if they had new tenants living in it by the first of February." That would be as close to a confirmation of severed ties with Stokely that Oscar could wish for. He took another bite of his sandwich and in a reply, that could have in response to her statement or the crab cake he said, "That hits the spot."

CHAPTER TWENTY-SEVEN

SUNDAY MORNING

The church was on Electric Street located in the far southwestern tip of the city. Stokely knew that by leaving his downtown apartment at 10:40 am and taking Jefferson Avenue as opposed to I-75, he would arrive late for the 11:00 am starting time. He hadn't been to church in years. He laughed aloud at the memory of his last church visit. A visit during which the pastor, the self-appointed Bishop Jenkins, tried feverishly in vain to push Stokely back while praying with his hand atop Stokely's forehead. Moments later, Stokely played dumb as Bishop Jenkins inquired whether he had accepted Jesus as his Lord and Savior. Stokely responded that he didn't differentiate between Jesus, Muhammad, or Siddhartha. That sent the bishop into a frenzy!

"Son," he looked to Stokely while wiping his brow of some type of curl activator and sweat. "Jesus is the onliest one who got up on the cross for yo' sins." Bishop Jenkins then segue into a monologue directed at Stokely but said in a manner that relied on input from the rest of the church.

"Mo' Ham-meds ain't got up on no cross!"

A few of the deacons chimed in with a well-timed, "Well!"

"Sid's Martha ain't knowed nuthin' 'bout raising on the third day!"

"Preach pastor! Tell 'em!"

"Son, you gots to 'cept Jesus fa' yo'sef. That's the onliest way yo' name gonna get written in the Book of Life," Bishop Jenkins said in a half-patronizing, half-pleading tone.

"I knows my name is in dere, ain't that right Mother Peterman?"

"Mine's in dere witcha!" Mother Peterman enthusiastically replied.

Wes sat in the back of the sanctuary shaking his head. He had coaxed Stokely into joining him that Sunday because a woman he was dating was participating in a Women's Day program. The service was inspirational in a The-Sistas-Praise-The-Lord-Too kind of way. But when Bishop Jenkins rose to begin the altar call, he targeted Stokely and Wes as the sinners in the congregation. He spoke from the pulpit but seldom took his eyes off the pair.

Stokely and Wes noticed. Wes assumed that his prospective girlfriend may have mentioned his coming to service. Stokely assumed that when the choir director was leading the choir through an energetic song that mentioned Jesus turning one's life around and he and Wes began laughing when the choir director instructed the choir to loop "And around and around and around." Then accompanied that repetitive singing with the eighteen-member choir jumping, and doing 360 degree turns in the air, Stokely couldn't keep his composure. Wes did the best he could because the woman he was dating was in the choir. But when the heavyset, off-key soprano only jumped 90 degrees to the left then back to the center then 90 degrees to the right - Wes let loose a round of hoots along with Stokely. Stokely was clearly the agitator.

When Bishop Jenkins announced, "Is there anyones who's ready to give themselves to tha Lawd?" Wes knew it would be some shit when Stokely rose. All the other people were regulars, Bishop could have let them go home. But Stokely had to extend service by heading to the altar. From the cold look, he received from the choir stand, Wes figured he hadn't made a good showing in church.

THE MEMORIES EASED Stokely's nervousness as he drove through the snow. By the time he turned off Schaefer, the parking lot was full and Electric Street was lined with cars. He smiled a bit when he saw Phoenix's Jeep.

Inside the church, Denise kept a close watch on the door. It was a draining effort to contain her excitement over Phoenix being interested in a man because she was a notorious one-and-done dater. After her dates, Phoenix would drive to Denise's house in Indian Village and complain. His teeth were too yellow. He was too consumed with material things. He didn't give to a charity. He alluded to not knowing his credit score. The list went on and on. One time Phoenix shared that a date asked if she was going to drink her water. She nodded 'No' and the date commenced to sticking his fingers in her water and then attempting to clean his nails. It was shocking and funny to hear Phoenix retell the incident. It was even more affirming that Phoenix adhered to her advice about driving herself to the first few dates. Phoenix told Mr. Nail-Cleaning she was going to the restroom and was probably miles away before he realized she wasn't returning.

Yet, the assurances that her daughter could conduct herself on a date did not abate Denise's fears that her daughter would never provide her with grandchildren. Denise was old-school in her thinking and hoped this guy could be 'The One' or at least provide her daughter with some pleasant memories.

Phoenix could see that her mother was more anxious than she was. When the choir finished their second selection, Phoenix began to kick herself for allowing her hopes to get so high. Just as doubt became a more darkened cloud over her wishes, Denise nudged her and nodded toward the sanctuary entrance.

The Greater Temple of The True Gospel was a close-knit church. They proclaimed to have 500 members; yet, often failed to mention that 350 of them were inactive, deceased, or in some other way not returning. Reverend Jericho Daniels was the pastor and his wife, Delores, had been Denise's roommate at Grambling.

Odd as it may seem, there is a socioeconomic stratification in the Black community when it comes to churches. Rarely, will professional people be spotted in what could be called a store-front church. True Gospel was not technically a storefront anymore since they moved from Visger Street. They currently occupied a standalone building that even had a steeple. But the mindset of the church could be considered spooky-religious. The type of church where if a member left before the benediction, they were made to feel as they were going to hell. Denise didn't really fit in, nor did she really care. She was a member because of her friendship with Delores. Denise considered Sunday morning church attendance more of ritual with greater value that any adherence to the gospel according to Reverend Daniels.

IT TOOK a moment for Stokely's eyes to adjust from the bright glare of the snow to the lighting in the sanctuary. But in time shorter than that, Denise sized him up and considered his worthiness for continuing to date her baby. He appeared nearly six feet tall, so if he is the one there is a 50 / 50 chance her grandson may inherit Stokely's height. She wasn't sure if he didn't intentionally shave or if he was growing a beard, but the facial hair gave her hope that he wasn't one of those tight-assed, no-facial-hair-wearing-because-they-want-White-folks-comfortable corporate types. His complexion was a deep brown, so Nana would be satisfied. He removed leather gloves from his hands and draped a wool dress coat over his arm, evidence that he has been somewhere before. Denise laughed when grown men wore brightly colored outfits to church that were better suited for a nightclub. She laughed harder when those men wore bubble jackets atop those bright suits looking like oversized little boys whose mothers underestimated the cold on Easter morning. Not that it was funny that brightly clad suit wearing brothers were coming to church - that's great; but just the sight of their fashion snafus tickled her.

While Stokely scanned the congregation for Phoenix, Denise had already decided he was handsome enough, tall enough, and possibly educated or cultured enough to merit a dinner visit to her home. Denise's wave caught Stokely's attention. Phoenix nudged Denise as hard as permissible and softly exclaimed, "Mom?!"

While accepting a bulletin from the usher and signaling the direction where he wished to sit, a seven-year-old boy with a round stomach, a clip-on tie, oversized white gloves, and a face gleaming from Vaseline rubbed all over, smiled at Stokely. With one arm extended and the other behind his back, the junior usher signaled for Stokely to follow him to a seat.

When he reached the pew, Phoenix stood and they hugged. He then reached across Phoenix to smile and shake her mother's hand. After the shake, Denise and Phoenix slid over so that

Stokely could sit at the end of the pew. Before he could sit, Reverend Daniels announced, "Can we have all the visitors stand and introduce themselves?"

Stokely was already standing. One other person on the other side of the sanctuary stood also. Seeing the other visitor was a woman, Stokely gestured for her to go first.

"Praise the Lord everybody!"

The congregation responded, "Praise the Lord."

She turned and smiled before stating, "Giving honor to God who is the head of my life. To Pastor and First Lady Daniels, I just want to say I'm glad to be in the house of the Lord one mo' time!"

While she was introducing herself, Stokely was stomped. Did he have to lead into his greeting with all that "Giving honor" stuff? It sounded scripted. What if he forgot his lines? He glanced nervously to Phoenix who was paying attention the other's woman's monologue.

"I'm so glad to worship here with y'all at The Greater Temple of the True Gospel dis mo'ning for the scriptures say when one or two are gathered in my name!"

The congregation hollered a collective "Amen!"

"So shall I be among them!" The woman then spasmed as if struck by electric jolt. "Oh, Jesus!"

One member responded, "Take yo' time!!" and another shouted, "Let the Lord have his way."

Denise poked Phoenix and pointed to Stokely who was visibly fretting. They giggled.

"I am Sister Shirley Brown and Mother Sissie Mae invited me here this mo'ning and I jes' wanna say thank ya' sista. And I also wants ta share greetin's from The New Mount Moriah Tabernacle of Faith where Elder Earl Watkins is our pastor. On behalf of Elder Watkins and the New Mount Moriah family I just want to thank y'all fa' having me here today."

While clapping, the church turned to Stokely. He mustered-up his enthusiasm and began with an earnest "Good morning saints!"

"Mornin' brother!" they replied.

"Whew, got that right," he thought before continuing "And, um yeah, my name is Stokely Robeson and my girlfriend, Phoenix Ellison invited me here to worship this morning and I just want to say thank you Lord." For good measure, he even extended his arms upward with open palms.

At first, Phoenix was trying to keep from laughing, but when she heard "Girlfriend" her heart sank and her cheeks burned from blushing. Denise was sitting erect but doing the slightly concealed repeated elbow nudge to Phoenix.

Reverend Daniels got Stokely off the hook with an extended hello gesture and "Brother Robeson and Sister Brown, we at The Greater Temple of The True Gospel welcome you to service and hope that you find it fitting to join us again. Brother Robeson, if you're looking for a church home ..." and then on cue, the organist chimed in and the congregation sung

If you want to see
G-O-D
then G-T-T-G
is where you wanna be!

If Wes had been there instead of Phoenix, Stokely surely would have doubled over in laughter. But instead he exhaled a long sigh while sitting down and turned to a surprised Phoenix. He was about to inquire with a "What did I say?" when he remembered he said, "Girlfriend." At that moment, he wished he could sink into the pew and vanish. But God wasn't granting those types of miracles. So instead he burned with delightful embarrassment like a schoolboy whose favorite teacher had kissed him on the forehead.

CHAPTER TWENTY-EIGHT

LATE SUNDAY MORNING

"This is cute," Oscar stated while entering the dining area from the master and only bedroom in the townhouse. Tanya's excitement showed as she rambled, "The glass two seater table with the handcrafted iron base could go right here. From this area, I can see the television that will go on that wall while also feeling a fresh breeze from the patio behind me." Tanya sound more like a realtor than a wife. But she wasn't exactly selling the place, she was selling her stake of independence.

Sometimes an easy endeavor is muddled by timing and circumstance. Tanya's desire to maintain her job was easily understood by Oscar. Her fiery professionalism had won her an executive position. Something he never quite put into words but was a tremendously significant matter to him was how attractive he found her when she was in work mode. Challenges and accomplishment brought out a lioness-like sexiness that he absolutely adored. He loved that about her. He supported her career and the supplemental matters that facilitated her career growth.

What he needed more selling on was whether things were over with her and Stokely and could the time he and Tanya were apart leave an opening for Stokely's return. Oscar was not convinced. Tanya mistook his displays of faint amusement as a hard adjustment to her staunch position of keeping her job.

As he entered the kitchen area and leaned on the counter, he cleared his throat and shared, "Your little friend has been hired by the MRO. They seem to be quite impressed with him. Differently than the way he impressed you or maybe the same, who knows?"

Tanya was stunned by the topic and excited for Stokely. She leaned against a nearby wall to appear relaxed but really to keep herself from falling over from a sudden case of lightheadedness.

Oscar assessed that he had Tanya's attention and continued, "I've been a trustee with the MRO for ten years and Mr. Robeson is the most impressive young architect I've encountered. It makes me feel ... what's the word? Awkward. Yes! That's it. It makes me feel rather awkward that as the most senior African American in the organization that to keep cool I must remain distant from the newly-hired and long-overdue African American youngster. You know what I mean by awkward? Have you ever felt awkward in this manner?"

Tanya took several deep breaths. She swallowed hard and with fragile conviction and a low tone, replied, "I feel awkward right now."

"You damn sure should!" Oscar shouted as he slammed his palm on the countertop. "You are goddamned right it's awkward," Oscar stated icily but with less volume.

Tanya was shaken. Oscar had never yelled at her. Her increasing fear matched the burning reddening of his face.

Oscar started clapping his hands in a patronizing manner. "There she is everybody. The Mrs., the woman who uses her husband's money to bankroll her sex-capades with her young lover. Mrs. Rousseau, how the hell do you dance around the principal facts?"

In a potent mix of hostility, disdain, and sarcasm, he pointed directly at Tanya and yelled, "I want you to have the damn job, whippee! And this townhouse - shit yeah! It's soooo cute." Oscar clasped his hands together and batted his eyes with mock femininity. Then he proceeded. "I want you to enjoy it. But how are you going to pretend that you weren't fucking somebody else? Shit, living with somebody? And then a muthafucking abortion?!!"

Oscar's voice was at a feverish pitch, "WHAT THE FU..."

He reached for his chest and gasped loudly.

Tanya, who had been staring at floor like an embarrassed child, turned sharply.

"Oscar? Baby? Oscar, are you alright?" She rushed toward the kitchen.

Oscar supported himself with the countertop. His face was flush red as he began taking short breaths with his eyes wide open. By the time, Tanya draped her arms around him and began rubbing his back, he had extended his inhaling and exhaling. His eyes began to water but he gained steady control of his breathing.

Tanya was frantic. She dashed for her purse to retrieve her phone. But in a whispery voice, Oscar waved her off. "I'm fine. This happened a few weeks ago. I'm okay, I just need to catch my breath." His wheezing was lessening.

Tanya looked to her phone, back at Oscar, and then to the phone again. "Tanya I'm okay. Put the phone away." He panted. "Let's go. Let's, let's ..." he took a deeper breath. "Let's just get a little something to eat."

Tanya was shaking as she returned and wrapped an arm around Oscar's waist to keep him steady. He handed her the keys and said faintly, "This is a really cute place. I can't wait to see how you fix it up." His smile was weak but well-intended. Tanya hit the auto start button on the Escalade's remote and locked the townhouse door behind them. She remembered that Oscar loved the nearby Morton's Steakhouse. If he wouldn't let her call for help, she figured she would nurse or at least keep close watch over him for the next few days.

Once inside the SUV, Tanya looked over at Oscar who although teary eyed seemed to have regained normal breathing. At that moment, she was cognizant of their age difference. She had taken Oscar's health for granted but after today and whatever happened a few weeks ago, the seed was planted in the far corner of her mind's garden - maybe she should return to Nashville.

Oscar could feel her looking at him. His chest was a little sore but he didn't want her to worry. He made another attempt at consoling her, "C'mon dear, let's eat." Using the rear viewing camera, Tanya began to back out of the parking space.

"Dear?" Oscar asked.

"Yes honey, what do you need?"

"You don't need to email or text anyone, do you?" he began to snicker.

Tanya laughed with him, "No, the person I need to communicate with the most is right beside me."

Oscar smiled and Tanya proceeded to make a way through the snow.

CHAPTER TWENTY-NINE

SUNDAY AFTERNOON

Stokely's ears were burning as he trailed Phoenix and Denise along northbound I-75 towards downtown. He knew he was the subject of their conversation. He was also thinking that if Phoenix aged in the same way as her mother, her future would be brighter and brighter. He was taken aback by their similarities in looks, speech, and just about everything else. Save for the facts that Denise is a few shades darker, wears a shorter hair style, and has a fuller ass, they could be easily taken for twins.

Denise inquired, "So he is a professor?"

"Really, he is an adjunct professor. He went to college and grad school to be an architect. For our date yesterday, he took me to a site that he is supposed to redesign for his new job that starts tomorrow," Phoenix responded.

"Does he have any kids? Babies' mamas? Or anything like that?"

"He didn't mention kids and doesn't seem to be the type

who would neglect them if he had them. I don't think he has any."

Denise added that to her approval checklist with an asterisk. She needed additional confirmation.

"He is coming out of a relationship with a live-in girlfriend," Phoenix surrendered cautiously. She opted to omit that the ex-girlfriend was married. She didn't want her mother to hold that against him.

"Oh! He was shacking! He isn't a freeloader, is he? Looking for a sponsor or something?"

"No ma, Stokely doesn't give off that vibe at all. I mean, I haven't even known him a week but he was willing to visit and talk with some of my B.B.D. girls."

Denise contemplated that for a moment and chose to add it to the pluses column of her Stokely assessment.

STOKELY WAS SORTING through his impressions of Denise. Besides her physical beauty, she seemed to be a peaceful soul. She didn't really fit in at that church. She gave off a pleasant distant-ness to the others except the pastor's wife. They appeared to be old friends. Even as Stokely shook hands with Reverend Daniels, he could see the pastor's wife and Denise sizing him up.

Phoenix looked good as usual. She has a way of making him happy without doing anything except being nearby. Just in their few times together - he wasn't sure if those times counted as dates - he recognized that whenever they hug, he loves to smell her hair. He could not pin a category. It wasn't fruity or sweet, but it was pleasant like a flower. He breathed it in big gulps.

DENISE BEGAN FISHING A LITTLE HARDER. "Are you two lovers?"

"MOM! No!" Phoenix shouted while exiting onto eastbound I-94. "Why would you ask me that?"

Denise was mildly relieved but answered "The way you were glowing and holding his arm after church. You two seem so familiar."

Phoenix was happily embarrassed.

Denise continued, "The good news is that he was cheesing and blushing just as much you. Y'all were sickening!" They both laughed before Denise continued, "But seriously it's nice to see that the feelings are mutual between you two. It's when the feelings are imbalanced, that someone is bound to end up heartbroken."

Denise cast a reflective gaze out the window, "Trust me, I know." After a long pause, she resumed more softly, "In all the years I spent with your father, we, I mean he never had that giddiness you and Stokely share." There was an even longer pause. "I always held these fantasies about how happy we could be. I know he liked me, cared for me; but I was never sure he loved me." There was a faint trembling in her voice. "I kept thinking, once he gets this gift or once we do this thing he is going to love me forever." It seemed now that Denise was speaking to herself. "One more thing, one more time, one more memory went from dating to a courthouse marriage to parenthood - at each step, I continued to tell myself 'when this happens, he is going to love me.'"

She turned to Phoenix, "I am so glad that God blessed me with you because otherwise I would have broken to pieces knowing I invested so much into someone who reciprocated so little. You were and always have been my greatest treasure. I swore to be a stronger woman for you. It took me a long time to make peace with the years I invested into making a relationship with your father. I had to learn that those years weren't worth the years I was sacrificing if I didn't accept that I couldn't make a man be where his heart isn't."

A few tears had escaped. Phoenix sighed, "Oh ma, I didn't ..." Denise cut her off, "No, you don't owe any apologies. I'm just saying what I should have long ago." She caught the few tears with her fingers. "It would be easy to make your father the villain. Indeed, he could have said something, done something ..." Denise shook her head. "Maybe he did and I couldn't hear it because I was so consumed with what I thought I could make happen." After a long pause, "Your father ... when he left it was like, like," she took a deep breath, "emancipation."

Phoenix exited I-94 onto Van Dyke as Denise continued, "I had spent maybe the last year or two before he left wallowing in pity and feeling embarrassed. I'm glad you were too young to remember, but Nana and Auntie Gladys held me together in those first few years. I was afraid that Nana would say, 'I told you so' but she never did. I've always loved my mother and aunt, but those years were so vital and important to where I am, where we are today that my love and appreciation for them is beyond measure." Denise smiled, "You didn't know bringing a cute guy to church would do all this to your mama?" They both laughed. Denise pushed a button on the radio, more to signal that she was done with that conversation than any desire to listen to music.

AS HE FOLLOWED Phoenix onto Vernor, Stokely admired the beauty of the homes in Indian Village. He thought of all the attention paid to the Detroit's decaying buildings and wished more could be said for Detroit's resilience as reflected in enclaves like this. Then it struck him, "Maybe that's an added dimension for Phoenix's book!"

As they turned onto Burns Street, Stokely slowed to a crawl thinking he would park in front of the home where Phoenix had pulled into the driveway. He then thought about cars sliding on the slush and smashing into his truck. As the ladies began to hop out of Phoenix's Jeep, he pulled behind them in the driveway. He quickly parked, hopped out, locked the door, and rushed over to the ladies to help them through the snow.

"Ms. Ellison, if you have a shovel in the garage I can shovel for you."

Denise was happily taken aback. She contained her impression and replied, "Thank you. There's nothing in the garage except my car. Last year, some no-good hoodlums broke-in and made off with some stuff I'd been storing in there. They probably would have robbed the house too if BooBaby wasn't here."

As they stepped towards the side door, Phoenix exclaimed, "Wait 'til you meet BooBaby, she is so precious!" Stokely was looking confused as Denise fetched the keys. Phoenix explained, "BooBaby is mama's dog and she is so sweet! Everyone loves BooBaby!"

With Phoenix's words, Stokely began to picture a Cocker Spaniel, a Pomeranian, or a little Yorkie. The Yorkie stuck in his mind as the breed Denise would have. He could visualize Denise curled on the sofa with a little Yorkie nearby.

When Denise swung the door open, up jumped a one hundred pound Rottweiler. Stokely was startled and exclaimed a "Hhheeeeeeeyyyyyy!" as BooBaby hugged Denise. As big as BooBaby was, she didn't knock Denise over - this greeting was an established ritual for them. Phoenix stepped behind her mother who was showering BooBaby with baby talk.

BooBaby hooked her front laws into the crooks of Denise's

elbows. Denise who had set aside her purse and keys upon the hallway table, took BooBaby's head into both of her hands while cooing, "Did the baby miss mommy? Mommy missed the baby. My BooBaby looks so hungry. Are ya hungry BooBaby? Is my baby hungry? Let's get that good girl something to eat. You want to eat BooBaby?"

Disconcerted by BooBaby's size and the completely off-based assumption about her breed, Stokely remained outside in the doorway. Phoenix reached back, "Don't be scared, BooBaby is okay. She sees that you are with us. She won't bother you. If you're cool, she'll be cool." Stokely swallowed a huge gulp and stepped cautiously inside.

Phoenix reached for the dog leash and hooked it onto BooBaby's extravagant collar. The collar had a big pink bow on it which matched the pink sweater jacket thingy Phoenix grabbed while waiting for Denise and BooBaby to finish their greeting.

"Now you be a good BooBaby while Phoenix and Mr. Stokely take you outside. Ok baby? Are you ready to go outside?"

The irony that such an intimidating dog had a pink jacket with a matching collar and was being fussed about like a toddler almost prompted Stokely to laugh but he didn't want to be disrespectful. After donning her jacket, BooBaby gave Stokely a thorough sniffing before wagging her approval. As they began to make their way down the driveway, Denise instructed, "Don't have my baby out there too long with nothing on her paws!" Feeling secure that he was out of earshot, Stokely began snickering. Both Phoenix and BooBaby looked at him incredulously.

"You better not be laughing at BooBaby," Phoenix warned.

"No, I'm not laughing at BooBaby. It's just I was expecting some little cuddly thing not a big ole Rottweiler!"

"BooBaby is cuddly," Phoenix replied with playful defiance while reaching to hold Stokely's hand. They proceeded out the driveway and began walking towards Jefferson Ave. Through the bay window in her living room, Denise smiled while watching the trio, Stokely and Phoenix holding hands and Phoenix holding BooBaby with the leash. The sight warmed Denise immensely.

CHAPTER THIRTY

LATER SUNDAY AFTERNOON

When they returned, Denise was waiting at the side door with a shovel and a broom.

"Phoenix can you get BooBaby inside and feed her? I bet she's starving after y'all done walked her to Canada." They all chucked. "Stokely can you grab the deep fryer I set at the bottom of the basement stairs and bring it outside, 'round the back?"

A few minutes later after lifting the heavy contraption up the stairs and through the snow, he saw Denise near the rear of the yard signaling for him to bring the fryer over to a spot she had cleared. Once he sat it down, she said, "While you're shoveling, I'm going to deep-fry a turkey. Would you like that?"

"Hell yeah! I mean, I'm sorry. Yes, Ms. Ellison, I would love that."

Denise laughed, then asked. "Okay, can you do Mrs. Height's next door too? She's ninety-four and what I do for my yard, I do for hers too."

"Sure, that's no problem. Ninety-four? Wow, I bet she has some stories to tell."

"She sure does. If you stick around maybe you will get to hear some of them." With that she turned her attention to prepping the fryer which communicated to Stokely he should begin shoveling. While clearing the area in front of the garage, he could see through the window that Phoenix was busy inside the kitchen as Denise went back and forth from the house to the pit. In his mind, he figured that if Phoenix has a willingness to cook, she is a keeper and if she is a good cook he may have to get going on his engagement ring strategies.

"MS. ELLISON, DINNER WAS DELICIOUS!"

"Thank you, but I only fried the turkey. That dressing, macaroni and cheese, and kale you devoured, Phoenix made those."

Stokely added, "Wow, Phoenix! It was awesome. It truly makes the diner want to kiss the chef."

Denise said, "So what are you waiting for?"

Stokely leaned over, kissed Phoenix softly on the cheek, and Denise interrupted, "That's thanks enough." Further intensifying Phoenix's welcome embarrassment.

Stokely rose from his seat at the dining room table and attempted to clear the table to which Denise responded, "I'll take care of that." She politely gathered the plates while being followed by BooBaby as she headed towards the kitchen.

"Are you excited about your new job tomorrow?" Phoenix inquired.

"Yeah but I can't really focus on it too much."

"Why not? You seemed excited yesterday."

"I am. But tomorrow afternoon, my parents and I are going to visit my sister."

"Visit your sister?"

"Yeah, I guess we haven't talked about it. It isn't much to talk about. My sister is locked-up at the Huron Correctional Facility in Ypsilanti. She's done twenty of her twenty-five-year sentence."

Phoenix eyes widened with curiosity and sadness. "Twenty-five years?"

"You know how sometimes mothers and daughters butt heads?"

Phoenix nodded.

"My mom was adamant about Song; my sister's name is Songhai and we call her Song for short - my mom didn't like Song dating this dude. He was a knucklehead. One of those punks who go overboard in trying to prove they're hard. My mom hated him. My dad never met him to which my mom would tell Song, 'if you too ashamed to introduce him to your father, then you shouldn't be seeing him.' Song was impressed by the little gifts he bought her; yet, she kept telling my parents that they were just friends. Well, long story short, Song was driving his car and waiting for him when he got into an argument with someone in the liquor store. Man-Man, that's dude's name, shot old boy and returned to the car. Song, naive and impressionable, drives him away from the crime scene. She was charged with second degree murder and Man-Man got life."

"Our lives were changed just like that," Stokely snapped his fingers.

Phoenix was speechless.

"A little girl trying to show her mother she knows how to deal with boys gets dealt one the unfairest hands ever. My parents were devastated. I felt hollow, like my soul had emptied. I don't think any of us ever accepted it. It's just a void you live with hoping it'll change. Tomorrow afternoon will be the first time we've seen her since the day after Christmas."

Stokely fumbled around with his glass before continuing, "That's why I admire what you do with BBD. I mean my sister was a good girl, really good grades, and very pretty. Popular in school and all that. Then a simple mistake that I bet a lot of teenagers make, changed her whole life. When I was talking to your girls, I was also wondering whether a program like yours could have been a difference maker for Song."

Stokely began choking back a bit and then eventually concluded, "One of the ironically fucked up parts about the ordeal was that Song was sentenced on what should have been the morning of her prom. Most of our family friends were seeing their children off to prom in tuxedoes and pretty dresses and we ..." Stokely took a deep breath. "We saw Song off to prison in those orange jumpsuits as opposed to a beautiful prom dress. It was the worse day of my life."

After a long pause, Phoenix clasped her hands around his and whispered, "I'm sorry Stokely." A few seconds later, she asked "Is there a chance for parole?"

"Yeah. She may make parole later this year. A couple years back, she was denied and my mom was crushed again. My dad, you could have knocked him over with a feather - he was shell shocked again. It's like we're trying not to get our hopes up but at the same time praying that Song can come home."

DENISE HAD BEEN EAVESDROPPING from the next room. She had to keep herself from crying while counting the blessing of never having to have that experience as a parent. The empathy she felt while listening further enhanced her good impression of Stokely.

CHAPTER THIRTY-ONE

MONDAY MORNING

Nomads traversing the desert undergo long intervals without water. When they come to an oasis, they fill themselves, their canteens, and their camels with water. When they resume their journey, they vigilantly ration their water because sometimes they are unsure when or where they will encounter the next oasis.

As she lay in her bunk, Song partook in a small ration of optimism by looking forward to the oasis of hope that accompanied each visit from her family. It took years to come to peace with the unfairness of her sentence, the guilt from the repercussions her choice had on her family, and the disappointment that came with relinquishing the dreams she had for herself.

Prior to meeting Man-Man, she was in the running to be the valedictorian of Benedictine High School. She had already accepted a full academic scholarship to Spelman. She imagined that she would have married a Morehouse man and probably would have been a mother and a CPA. Then she met Man-Man. He wasn't even cute. He was simply her life's forbidden fruit. For all the years she had been teased as "Miss Perfect," her dalliance with Man-Man was to show everybody ... what? Show them what? That she wasn't perfect? That she could play with the bad boys and come away unscathed? That she was smarter than her mother? What the hell was she thinking?

Song figured that doubt and disappointment were two sides of the same coin of misery allocated to her by the "Get tough on crime" judge. Other inmates told her that there are only two days to a jail sentence - the first and the last days. If that were true, she estimated that perhaps she had reached the dawning of the second day after a hellaciously long evening from the first day. No matter which way it's dressed, twenty years is a long fucking time. As with the previous seven thousand one hundred forty-six sunsets, she cursed both Man-Man and the day they met.

IN THE THREE HOURS, she had been mired down at her desk, Phoenix was pushing ahead with unbridled enthusiasm. She was motivated by the thought that "This grant could be the big one." Building Beautiful Daughters had been surviving on a piecemeal budget of small grants, donations, and sheer will. This grant would provide some fiscal peace of mind while enhancing the services BBD provided. Perhaps feverishly or "In a zone" would better describe Phoenix's productivity until she was startled by her ringing phone.

Regina's voice came through the receiver, "Phoenix, are you sitting down?"

"I can be. Is everything alright?"

"Starkeisha, Phoenix. Star was escorted out of school by protective services."

"Oh, no no no." Her next words had to work around the lump of sadness in her voice. "What happened?"

"You are sitting, right?"

"Yes, what happened Regina?"

"She stabbed her mother."

"WHAT?!"

"Yeah. I didn't want to believe it either. But it's true."

"Awww no, Regina. Are you sure?"

"When she came in this morning, Star told me they had a fight. Her mother accused Star of flirting with her man, so she jumped on her. Star fought back and they had a bit of a shoving match before her mother punched her in the nose. After she stopped the bleeding and hid in the bathroom for an hour or so, she found her mother sprawled out on the couch pissy-drunk. That's when Star stabbed her in the stomach."

"Oh, my God ..."

Starkeisha had endeared herself to Phoenix in a kind of root-for-the-underdog way. Her grades did not reflect her intelligence. Inside and outside of the classroom, she typically kept to herself. What bothered her most was the inordinate and often inappropriate attention she got. Star had a figure that a twenty-five-year-old would envy, but she was only fourteen. People treated her as if she were woman and far too many men attempted to proposition her, especially her mother's boyfriends. She developed a shield to keep people from getting close to her. The first few weeks of the school year, Star demonstrated an extreme reluctance towards any of the BBD activities. But in time, BBD became a haven, the one place where she could be her age.

Phoenix inquired, "How is her mother?"

"She's not dead or the police would have come or something. This kind of reminds me of the thing you told me your mother said about dumb mamas."

Phoenix managed a morose laugh. She had shared with Regina what Denise told her one day when she was venting about some of troubles the students face at home. Denise had replied, "You know you could have a dumb daddy or even no daddy for that matter, things may be hard but you stand a chance. But if you got a dumb mama, you're doomed! Only Jesus can save you!" Phoenix repeated Denise's colloquialism to insert a little humor into a sad conversation. They managed a slight chuckle before Regina responded, "If anyone has a dumb mama, it's Star. Lord knows we need a miracle right now. I'll call you later when I find out what happens next."

"Alright, talk with you later," Phoenix said as she ended the call.

"FIRST, Stokely's sister and now possibly Star," thought Phoenix as she stepped down from the stool at her desk and walked toward the window. She thought back to a conversation she had a few weeks ago about the rising number of Black women in prison. The scariest thought was how the imprisoned women were often in their predicament due to the direct or indirect influence of men, kind of like Song and Man-Man. Star avoided her mother's boyfriend's advances only to end up in fight with her mother and now she is being introduced to the system. "She must have been plenty scared to stab her mother." Phoenix was thinking while gazing out of the window.

"It sure is a gloomy morning."

CHAPTER THIRTY-TWO

MONDAY

Ypsilanti is approximately forty miles west of Detroit but the Robeson's drive to the prison felt like much longer journey. To lighten the mood, Cleve, Stokely's father's name was Cleveland but nearly everyone called him Cleve, inquired about Stokely's morning at his new job.

"It has pluses and minuses. The minus is that it is a part-time consultant gig. When I hear 'part-time' I interpret it as the executives intentionally avoiding benefit packages."

A truth to which Cleve replied, "Preach!"

Elaine, Stokely's mother, sat in the rear of Stokely's crew cab truck. She appeared dazed as she stared out the window with a consistent daze that she has held during each of the prison visits for the last twenty years. Behind each daze is the memory of her precious little girl, her shopping partner, and her pint-sized look-a-like. She never stopped kicking herself for not telling Cleve sooner. It all happened so fast, as far she could calculate, Song couldn't have known Man-Man much more than a few weeks, maybe a month. The gifts and the attention shouldn't have mattered because Song got all the attention one girl could handle from Cleve. As a baby, the bottoms of all her shoes were as good as new because Cleve wouldn't put his little doll baby down. He had to carry her everywhere just for spoiling's sake. He'd boast, "Why have little girl babies if you can't spoil 'em?" Song was spoiled, not a brat, but definitely favored.

Every day, Elaine pondered what she could have done better or differently to prevent the incarceration of her oldest child. Cleve had his own worries compounded by keeping watch over Elaine. In some ways, caring for Elaine was a diversion that kept him from being swallowed by the despair of Song's circumstances. Doubts of whether he overdid or didn't do enough gnawed at his spirit.

"On the other hand, my position is a new effort by the MRO, so they are sort of sticking their toe in the water before getting in any deeper," Stokely confided.

"Well, they better get their life jackets because their gonna get caught in a Robeson undertow!" Cleve nearly shouted as they exchanged high fives.

Their joviality prompted a small smile from Elaine. It always made her heart glad to see her men happy. She was so proud of Stokely. The choice to transfer Stokely away from Benedictine after Song's arrest may have been a lifesaving choice because she and Cleve were afraid that cloud of depression that overtook their home was going to choke the life out of Stokely. A new school and an opportunity to define himself separately from his sister was a shot of positive energy that reversed his descent into despondency, plus he was introduced to architecture. Who knew his fortunes would change so drastically? Now if he could only do something about shacking with that married hussy. He thinks she doesn't know, but a mother always knows - especially if she married to a co-pilot like Cleve.

"The pluses are that I can work any twenty hours I choose

in a week and I have full creative freedom to design three renderings of varying scopes and costs."

"Sounds like the start of something special," Elaine said on a congratulatory tone.

"It is. They tossed a softball pitch to a home run hitter," Stokely stated confidently as they all laughed.

~

THE CONVERSATION at the table was light. The usual updates and gossip led to Song surprisingly asking Stokely, "So when are you going to settle down bruh?"

Stokely stammered with shock, "Well, yeah, you know, hey, I was thinking ..."

Elaine's ears perked and Cleve folded his arms across his chest while leaning back in his chair. Cleve, Elaine, and Song all waited for Stokely to continue. Song even wound her hand in a motion that said, "Go on."

"Me and Tanya broke up."

"Thank God" escaped Elaine's lips before she could catch herself.

"But I've met someone else."

Cleve was proud and incredulous, "Shit Stokely, you ain't wasting no time, are you?"

Song added, "Damn, you got it like that?"

"Nah, no. We met by coincidence. Her name is Phoenix and she runs this non-profit that helps middle and high school girls. I've even met her mother and had dinner at her mother's house."

"So that's why you don't have time to call your own mother?" Elaine chimed.

Cleve inserted, "This is a record for you isn't it son? Were you even single three days?"

Song was nodding in agreement, "That is pretty swift Stokely."

"First, Tanya left me," Stokely asserted trying to grab this conversation bull by the horns.

"She did you a favor!" Elaine added with an eagerness that garnered a warning glare from Cleve. "I'm sorry baby, but living with a married woman? How could you?"

"You knew she was married?"

"Look boy, I didn't get this old being no fool."

Stokely looked to Cleve for verification.

"Don't go looking to your father either. Look here, I'm the one who taught you the value of loving dark skinned women. But with dark skinned folks, it's easier to spot the tan line from the wedding band."

Stokely was a little surprised but then shook his head at his mother's resourcefulness.

Elaine continued, "I liked her until she was helping me clean up after the Labor Day cookout. We were joking about Cleve needing to give you more practice time on the grill when she went to wash the dishes. I dried them and when I handed her the towel to dry her hands, my suspicions were confirmed."

Stokely and Song leaned in closer to their mother. Cleve smiled the "Even-I-Can't-Fool-This-Woman" smirk.

"I'm going to tell you something else. Tanya, she did have strong feelings for you. But you were so in love with love, you didn't see the tentativeness behind her love. When a woman, a secure woman loves, and maybe even some of y'all men - I'm only sure about this one right here ..." Elaine gestured with her thumb toward Cleve. "But I was saying when a secure woman loves, there is a surrender involved. A type of let-go-and-see-what-happens type of thing. Sistergirl and all her professional accomplishment was either a control freak who was afraid of true love's need for surrender or holding back to keep from surrendering."

Stokely was becoming deflated by his mother astute analysis of Tanya.

Elaine reached across the table and patted him on the cheek, "Don't get all up in your turtle shell like you used to do when you were in trouble as a little boy. I'm just letting you know, that Tanya despite all her promise, just wasn't the one for you.

Elaine let Stokely's head emerge from his turtle shell before going on, "Now tell us about this new one who does the thing with the girls."

Stokely looked around the table at his family. Each member gave him a nod of understanding and a smile which encouraged him to proceed, "Well, like I said, I met Phoenix kinda coincidentally. She was visiting our offices and I was the only one there to answer her architecture questions."

Everyone nodded with warm smiles for him to continue.

"Then I guess I was meeting Tanya for the closure talk." He did the bunny ears / quotation mark gesture with both hands when he said closure talk. "When I got to the restaurant to meet Tanya, Phoenix was there with some other people and then we left together."

"Oh, hell nawl Stokely!" Song laughed. "I know you got a little smooth thing going but you ain't went nowhere to meet your ex and leave with your future boo, hell to the nizzawl!"

Cleve and Elaine were laughing.

Stokely laughed too. He then went on, "See I got mad at Tanya, so I walked away." He tilted his head and raised his eyebrows toward his mother as a curtsy to her admonition about not allowing his temper to cause him to put his hands on a woman. "Now I don't know what happened with Phoenix and her friends, but one of the guys was trying to get on and I guess she shot him down so he was outside with an attitude."

Cleve asked, "How do you know he had an attitude?"

"Easy, when I walked out the restaurant, I gently bumped into him and he shouted 'Motherfucker.'"

Song was nearly hysterical when she mocked him, "I gently bumped into him." The guards in the waiting room looked over and signaled for them to keep it down.

"Did you hit him?" Elaine asked sternly although she already knew the answer.

Cleve looked on with disapproval.

Stokely was busted. He opened his mouth to explain but before he could speak Elaine arched one eyebrow.

"I only punched him once."

Song was shaking her head trying to muffle her laughter. In her mind, she was picturing Stokely as a first grader punching kids in the choir while the choir was singing during Sunday service. She recalled how for the next few months, any activity that involved the choir required that Stokely stayed by her side. She laughed harder as she recalled his inability or unwillingness to take verbal sleights frequently led to him throwing punches. Later, he would adopt an innocent disposition to try to convince their parents that his anger was justified. Looking across the visitor's table, she could see her baby brother hadn't changed much at all.

Cleve sighed a disappointed, "C'mon Stokely. What if ...?"

Stokely finished Cleve's question, "... He had a gun?" Stokely caught himself before saying that he was packing. Instead he demurred and acquiesced, "You're right. I shouldn't have punched him. But this is about Phoenix, right?"

The others glanced at each other as if to say, "Yeah, that's right."

"PHOENIX," Stokely said with exasperated emphasis,

"Saw what happened, grabbed my arm to calm me down, and sort of walked me away."

"Yeah, 'cause I wasn't there to stand next to you," Song added with self-depreciating humor.

Stokely appreciated her wit, winked and pointed at her as he continued, "And we ended up walking to the casino."

Elaine looked at Cleve while shaking her head, "What are we going to do with him?"

"How far of a walk is that? In January? In Detroit?" Song asked in a flurry.

"About a mile or so. It was pretty mild that day so it wasn't too bad," Stokely confirmed.

Elaine took a deep breath and let out a long sigh.

Song added, "But dang, you just broke up with Tanya. Isn't it a little soon?"

Both Cleve and Elaine nodded in agreement. "Your sister is right. You can't go swinging from woman to woman like Tarzan on some vines." Stokely knew that Cleve was saying this both truthfully and as a measure of keeping the peace amid his mother and sister. They would have a different talk among themselves later.

"She sounds like a great girl and I want you to be happy. Can you just not burden her with the healing you need to do regarding Tanya?" Elaine asked. "It isn't fair to her to unknow-ingly be your bounce back girlfriend."

The guard announced that visiting time was over.

"I will."

They exchanged hugs and goodbyes. As they gathered to go their separate ways, Song took long look at her family. It was her last long swig of water from this oasis of a visit and marked the beginning of another journey across the penal desert toward the restorative feelings that will come with the next family visit.

CHAPTER THIRTY-THREE

TUESDAY

Oscar caught the first flight back to Nashville on Tuesday morning. He was proud of himself for remaining cool in welcoming Stokely during his first morning with the MRO. Oscar even found it amusing that both were watching Edna switch as she walked down the corridor. He promised himself he would remain civil; yet, when he looked at Stokely he couldn't help but be reminded of him and Tanya.

The ideas Stokely expressed for the abandoned train tracks at the end of Dequindere were as imaginative as Dean Griffin predicted Stokely's ideas would be. Oscar figured that the renderings Stokely would devise would facilitate his fundraising with the Green Movement groups. If Stokely's production matched his talk, it wouldn't be long before he was a full-time employee. The conflict of his enthusiasm about Stokely's promise and his disdain for Stokely's relationship with Tanya caused Oscar to be happy for the refuge of returning to Nashville.

While unpacking his clothes and selecting those he would

wear on his return trip to Detroit for Friday night's black tie event, he missed a call to his cell phone. Looking at the number and figuring the area code implied that this was Tanya's new number he had yet to save, he pushed the return call button. When a female voice answered, his response came out before he realized he may have jumped the gun with his greeting, "Tanya, I missed your call. What's going on?"

Initially, he anticipated expecting a "Just thinking about you" or some other idle lover chatter. Instead, he got several seconds of silence.

Again, but this time he spoke a bit more tentatively, "Hey Tanya. Hello?"

"Is this Oscar Rousseau?"

"Yes, it is. I apologize. I was expecting a call from someone else. Who is calling?"

Phoenix's professional voice cracked into that of a nervous little girl, "Dad?"

It was Oscar's turn with silence.

For him, the moment felt comparable to standing near the edge of a subway platform as a train roars by at top speed. That was how Oscar felt as his mind rolled back the years of missed opportunities to be a father to his daughter.

He wanted to hang up out of shame. While at the same time, he was transfixed.

The shaken voice replied, "Dad. This is Phoenix."

Oscar began to gasp for breath while backing up to take a seat on the edge of the bed. Stammering to hold back the tears of shame, he replied, "Phoenix. Phoenix, yes, I know. It's you, Phoenix."

After what seemed much longer than the ten seconds that transpired, Phoenix broke the silence with a whispery inquiry, "Can I call you back at a better time?"

With a fragile softness, Oscar said while looking at himself trembling in the bedroom mirror, "Please Phoenix. Could you please call me back?"

"Ok." Then with a barely audible whisper, "Bye."

Oscar's lips mouthed, "Bye" but Phoenix had hung up by the time sound escaped his vocal chords. When he looked at the phone in his hands, his hands were trembling. As he glanced up toward the mirror, he could see that his face had reddened and tears were flowing. Seconds later, a loud guttural sob escaped the depths of his esophagus and echoed throughout the room.

Loving and working to forgive Tanya had been Oscar personal penitence for abandoning his family. Although Denise probably would give less than a damn to know that he thought he could absolve his guilt by marrying and being a better husband to someone else, Oscar needed Tanya to help him forgive himself. That's why he needed to forgive her for Stokely, to unshackle his anger and resume his own self-prescribed repentance.

Phoenix called her father on a whim. She spent the morning at Cleage Academy and had an hour to kill before she was expected to meet with administrators at Fred Shuttlesworth Middle School. For all the times, she kicked herself for letting days pass without calling, she had finally done it. It wasn't as bad as she thought. While listening to the hum of her engine as her Jeep warmed, she was thankful that her mother did not bind her down with bitterness. Instead, Denise coached her daughter towards suspending judgement until Phoenix could talk to her father herself. "Who knows?" Denise would say, "We should consider that his absence may have been better for us than his presence. Would you want to live with a father who did not want to live with you?

Phoenix remembered feeling perplexed during that conversation until Denise added, "His not wanting to live with us may have nothing to do with us. That is his choice. A choice that you and I can't take personally even though it impacts us directly."

Not many mothers talk to their pre-teens in that way, but those morsels of living without feelings of anger and rejection made the call to her father much easier. As she reached to put the Jeep in gear, she smiled knowing that her bashfulness on the phone was borne of awkward curiosity as opposed to bitterness. The irony was that a brief verbal exchange with her father would make her appreciate her mother more.

When she parked at Shuttlesworth Middle, she had a text from Stokely.

Stokely: How would you like to go to Baker's for dinner? I hear there is a really good band tonight.

She projected the length of the Shuttlesworth meeting and how much paperwork she wanted to finish at the office before figuring that she could get home, relax and freshen up for the 8 o'clock performance.

Phoenix: Great. Can you pick me up at 7:30?

She gathered her things and exited the Jeep. By the time she entered the school, she felt the vibration in her purse, she didn't need to read the text to know that Stokely would be there.

However, despite Denise's positive programming, the anticipation of gaining a new client, and the prospect of a wonderful night with Stokely - with each passing moment her call to Oscar released deep seated emotions that began to smear her optimism with a melancholic dread. Her repetitive thought became "That man abandoned me and my mother."

CHAPTER THIRTY-FOUR

TUESDAY EVENING

Their small table was directly in front of the stage. At first glance, the afroed lead singer, baby-faced drummer, and mellowed saxophonist could conjure memories of Abbey Lincoln, Max Roach, and Coleman Hawkins. Along with the intimacy of Baker's Keyboard Lounge and even the small amount of cigarette and cigar smoke that hung in the air, it seemed as if Stokely and Phoenix had warped back in time to the height of the jazz age.

The band, *Nzinga*, carried the lead singer's name as its moniker. Tonight's performance was dedicated to Angela Bofill. Stokely and Phoenix's proximity to the stage made it seem as if Nzinga was singing directly to them. As they sat, Nzinga was conveying the soulful support of Bofill's *I'm On Your Side*.

Rather softly, Stokely leaned over and asked, "Is everything okay?" He remained in the position for few seconds to inhale the sweetness of Phoenix's perfume.

Phoenix smiled warmly when she turned his way. Their faces were so close, that if they were strangers they would have been startled. Instead, with a delicately light peck, their lips touched before Phoenix replied, "I'm ok, Stokely." But the cocoa pools of her eyes widened with a mix of hope and traces of anguish.

The waitress set Phoenix's Amaretto Sour on the table alongside Stokely's Hennessy & Coke. He nodded a "Yes" to the inquiry of "Would that be all right now?" Stokely and Phoenix clinked their glasses as Nzinga crossed the song's bridge.

Stokely leaned back and draped his arm around the back of Phoenix's chair. Phoenix scooted her chair closer and as she settled, leaned her head back onto Stokely's shoulder. Stokely began lip syncing along with Nzinga with a very direct gaze into Phoenix's eyes.

While blushing from the attention, Phoenix blurted, "I talked to my father today."

Stokely thoughtfully demurred. He rubbed Phoenix's shoulder and kissed her on the forehead. "How do you feel now?"

"Not as relieved or happy as I thought I would." She pondered momentarily before resuming, "At first I was cool. But the more I thought about it, about him leaving me and my mother hanging, I started to feel bitter. Plus, judging from his response, I believe I caught him off-guard, maybe even shocked him."

Feeling unsure of how to reply, Stokely continued to rub her shoulder.

Nearly a minute later, "I thought talking to him would provide some type of resolution. That it would be exciting. But really it unearthed some sad feelings I'd been carrying for years."

Thinking this was more of a release or vent as opposed to a request for help or answers, Stokely took another sip of his drink while looking at Phoenix as an effort to show he was listening. It worked. She continued, "Would you believe that he was stammering like he was at a loss for words?"

Resisting the urge to answer quickly but seeking to lighten her spirits, Stokely answered, "You know, baby your voice is so captivating it could knock a pause into someone."

He smiled. She looked at him quizzically before smiling back "Knock a pause into someone? Ok Bernie Mac." They chuckled together.

Phoenix sipped her drink and sat erect as if being struck by an unusual thought. "Do you think it was as uncomfortable for him as it is for me?"

With both eyebrows reaching upward and a briefly pursed lip expression to show his contemplation of the idea but not letting on that she appeared to be repeating herself, Stokely responded, "Yeah, it probably could be."

As they reflected, Nzinga segued into Bofill's *Tonight I Give In*. Phoenix looked to Nzinga with a telepathic question about the song selection. Nzinga winked at her with a smile while continuing Bofill's impassioned yearning.

Stokely missed Phoenix's and Nzinga's exchange. As a man, he wouldn't understand that somethings between women are best unsaid.

CHAPTER THIRTY-FIVE

LATE TUESDAY EVENING

She broke the silence with an awkwardness fitting for a middle school girl, "Can you stay with me tonight? But not in THAT way, but just like, be there?" She turned abruptly to the window with body language that said she didn't want to listen. However, Stokely, relying on wisdom instilled in him by Cleve, knew she was listening and waiting.

"I can do that. Just tell me where I should park."

It could have been the truck's heating system blowing on full blast, but Stokely would wager confidently that he heard a sigh of relief.

Once inside, Stokely promised himself that this would not be his last visit to Phoenix's loft. He knew he would need the time to go through all her albums. While the shelving was floor to ceiling, her record collection went from the floor to about five feet. The upper shelves were lined with pictures of her, her and Denise, her and some of her friends, and even her and BooBaby. There were no pictures of her with another dude, Stokely noted. But right now, Phoenix's expansive record collection was calling him.

In surprised exasperation, Stokely said, "You even have them in alphabetical order and grouped by genre!" He was as excited as an alcoholic with free run of a distillery. Phoenix was amused at his delight.

"You got Donald Byrd's *Places & Spaces*!!" Stokely shrieked. That caused a series of chuckles from Phoenix. As Stokely's eyes roved the shelving where the other half of the wall was filled with books. "Hhheeeeeeyyyyy!" Stokely's happiness was palpable. He reached for the large Gordon Parks photo book, "Gordon is my man!"

"You know Stokely, all of those books and records will be here next time you visit."

"Oh, yeah, okay," he replied while returning the book to the shelf. Then he froze as he turned to face a rather large print of a Romare Bearden painting. "This is beautiful," he gasped slowly.

"Thanks," she said as motioned for him to follow her. As they made their way to the stairs, Phoenix reached for the bannister, balanced herself, and unzipped her boots. She slid them off and placed them beside the stairway. Noticing that the stairs were carpeted, Stokely assumed the loft area would also be carpeted, so he followed suit and removed his boots.

"Let me have your coat and sweater."

She took his things and hung them on the coat rack on the hooks next to hers. She reached for his hand and led him up the stairs to the loft area. The loft area was dominated by the large skylight window that gave view to a resplendently bright full moon.

As Phoenix laid on top of the comforter, she patted the center of the bed for Stokely to lay down. The pat-pat noise snagged Stokely's attention from staring at the moon. When he laid down on his back, his feet were still on the floor with his knees bent at the foot of the bed. Phoenix placed some of her overstuffed pillows on the floor and tugged at Stokely's shoulder for him to move up on the bed. As he settled in the center of the bed, Phoenix kissed him on the cheek and snuggled closely. She nestled into the crook of his shoulder and aligned the bridge of her nose just beneath his jawline near his ear. She draped one leg over his midsection while also unbuttoning one button on his shirt and bringing her palm to rest on the bare flesh of his chest.

Stokely mumbled, "Baby, you're like a cat."

Phoenix playfully purred, "Meow."

With his left hand and arm, he cupped her body and pulled her closer. He let his hand rest on her ass.

"Stokely?"

"Yeah, Phoenix?"

"Only my man can put a hand on my ass."

He squeezed her ass while definitively stating, "Honey, your man is here." To which the little wiggling of her bottom in his palm was her confirmation of agreement. This led Stokely to begin singing Freddie Jackson's *You Are My Lady* in a whisper.

There on Phoenix's bed, engulfed in lunar light, they were both asleep before Stokely could finish the song.

CHAPTER THIRTY-SIX

EARLY WEDNESDAY MORNING

Phoenix was already making breakfast smoothies in the kitchen when her iPod alarm clock awakened Stokely with the harmony of Erykah Badu singing about how she looks without makeup.

To Stokely, waking up in Phoenix's bed was comparable to waking up in heaven. As he lifted his head, he noticed the paisley print sticky note attached to the tent made in his pants from his erection. He reached for the note which read: "Seems like you're ready" followed by a happy face with its tongue out. "She is something else" Stokely thought while smiling.

"What are you smiling about?" said Phoenix as she sat on the edge of the bed. She extended a smoothie to him.

"You, us," Stokely replied while reaching for the drink.

Phoenix blushed a bit before continuing, "On another day, maybe I can cook you breakfast but this morning I have a standing appointment with my mom at the Y." She took a sip of her smoothie under Stokely's watchful eye. Then reluctantly, he followed his slow sip with wide-eyed delight. "This is good! What is it?"

Playfully, she answered, "You don't get all the secrets after one night. You got to put in some time before you get the goodies."

The double meaning wasn't lost on Stokely he shook his head before taking another sip.

"You got any special plans today?"

Stokely stood up, placed his drink on the nightstand, and stretched. "I'm going to switch my lease to a studio apartment a few floors down from where I'm staying now. I really haven't been in the mood for much apartment shopping, you know."

"I bet you're biding time before your next house."

Stokely pointed his index finger at her before saying, "Booyah! That's exactly what I'm doing." He took another sip. "I got to knock out a few office hours before my class and then swing by the new job and start laying some more groundwork there. Later on, I'm headed to Flood's where me and my guys get together to chop it up."

"Flood's? That's where my friend Regina and her band perform - I got to go see her perform. She talks about it all the time. You met Regina when you came to Cleage."

Stokely snapped his finger. "Damnit, that's why she looked so familiar. Yeah, you should see your girl perform, her and the band be turning it out!"

When he was a teen, Stokely confided in his father his confusion in dealing with his crush on a new girl who transferred into the class he shared with his old crush. To which Cleve asked, "How would I know if you had a hole in your sock right now?"

"Hunh?"

"Right now, you got yo' shoes on don't ya?"

Stokely nodded confused while looking at his feet for confirmation that his shoes were definitely on.

"Yo' big toe could be just wigglin' and gigglin' through a big ole hole in your sock but as long as you keep your shoes on, nobody is the wiser, right?" Cleve arched an eyebrow and nodded his head toward his son. The wisdom of his analogy flew over the boy's head.

Stokely looked at his father confused.

"Boy just keep yo' shoes on and everything will be alright. You gotta just let the sleeping dogs lie." Stokely was further confused.

Cleve exhaled deeply, "Just keep yo' damn mouth shut when it comes to talking to ladies about another woman. If pressed, parcel out the truth in tiny tidbits but do not and I mean DO NOT lie. Just enough truth to keep things moving without incriminating yourself. Are you following me son?"

Faint understanding started to seep into young Stokely's mind.

With both hands on Stokely's shoulders, Cleve said, "Son, some things are just better left unsaid. When the time comes, I hope you keep your toe wigglin' inside your shoe." Cleve winked and patted his son on the head.

STOKELY SIPPED the smoothie again thinking that regarding Gina, he was going to wiggle his toe inside his shoe. "Some nights your friend's band has the place rocking! It'll be real cool if you could come one night. Anyhow, what about your day? Any big plans?"

"I'm trying to land a new client. The more schools I work with, the better my chances to increase funding which leads to me offering better services."

Stokely initiated a high five that Phoenix slapped enthusiastically.

"Think we may be able to see each today?"

"Do you Facetime?"

"Occasionally, but then I can't smell your perfume."

"I don't wear much perfume."

"Well, I guess you just smell good naturally."

"Aww, thank you Stokely. But I use my own combinations of body oils and stuff."

"Like moonshine perfume?"

She slapped his arm, "No, silly. Look I gotta meet mom. Maybe we can grab lunch or if your guys don't mind, I can join y'all later." The she giggled again, "Moonshine perfume, you are a mess!"

They proceeded down the stairs and when they got to the bottom, Stokely sat and began lacing his boots. "You and your mom do like a spinning class or something?"

"We mix it up from it up from time to time," she said while grabbing her keys.

Stokely met her at the door where they engaged in an intimate hug. Stokely kissed her on the forehead before joking, "I'm not sure if our relationship is ready for morning breath."

Phoenix laughed as she pecked him on the lips and they made their way out the door.

CHAPTER THIRTY-SEVEN

WEDNESDAY MORNING

"Let me get this right. You like my program and how it can help your female students but you do not want to implement it because it does not serve your male students?"

Phoenix's incredulity was hot lava ready to erupt. Internally, she worked feverishly to tone down the intensity of her glare. Her contempt for Principal Wilkins was growing by the minute. She had heard about the bureaucratic ineptitude of some school leaders and was convinced that Principal Wilkins could be the poster-child for "Muthafuckers in the way of progress."

Wilkins replied, "The way Mrs. Chisholm described your program Miss Ellison, she went on and on about what it could do. Trust me, she was very impressed from your presentation and convinced me that what your program could do would make a difference. However, she failed to mention that it only serves one half of our student body. I cannot in good conscience endorse your program without thinking of all of the children at Shuttlesworth."

With that, he smirked in a manner that implied he would not budge from his position.

Phoenix took a deep breath, visualized overturning his desk, but instead, extended her hand for a shake. Principal Wilkins gave the limp-wet-fish handshake that all but eradicated the last vestiges of respect Phoenix had for him.

When she exited the outer office, and began buttoning her coat before leaving the building, Mrs. Chisholm was standing across the hall shaking her head in disbelief.

"He turned you down."

Phoenix nodded affirmatively.

"That ole yassa-boss negro can't stand anything innovative. If I know him, he probably shot down the program because of you. He is intimidated strong women, especially young ones."

Phoenix just shook her head. Principal Wilkin's rejection of BBD was a setback. BBD's roster of clients consisted of Cleage Academy, three girl scout troops, and two church youth ministries. Without the addition of some big clients who would provide access to 50 to 100 new girls, Phoenix's prospects of securing additional funding was shrinking. Could she even afford to maintain this rate of services another year with the same level of revenue?

Mrs. Chisholm continued in a consoling manner, "Miss Ellison?" She waited for Phoenix to look her in the eye, "The scriptures tell us 'do not become weary in doing good, for at the proper time we will reap a harvest if we do not give up.' These children need programs like yours, don't be discouraged."

Phoenix's feelings of defeat must have been obvious because Mrs. Chisholm shifted into full maternal mode.

"I'll call my good friends over at Youthville and Church Terrell Academy and put in a good word for you. I'll email you an update, ok?"

Mrs. Chisholm's hospitality and good intentions got Phoenix to smile.

"I appreciate your help Mrs. Chisholm."

With that they shared a goodbye hug and Phoenix lifted her scarf to cover her nose and mouth as she opened the door to a blistery wintry morning.

THE RUMOR WAS SPREADING like wildfire throughout the building. Some of the holdovers from the takeover with Diamler carried a cynicism that could be infectious. While the rumored layoff wasn't expected to impact as many employees as the 2001 Chrysler layoffs, had the IT manger did a corporate snoop on the emails sent that day, they would have noticed a plethora of forwarded resumes. Working for an automotive company in Detroit could be akin to playing Russian roulette, while the last trigger-pull of layoffs may have spared one's employment livelihood, each spin of the chamber brought about its own feelings of impending doom.

The proverbial ink on Tanya's new lease had not dried; yet, she began forecasting scenarios where she would have to break it and move to Nashville. Since Monday, the rumor had transformed from layoffs to reassignments. Those who had been with the company through Diamler, Cerebus, and now Fiat carried dark, bruised-looking, emotional bags under their eyes of hope. They had survived three spins of the roulette wheel, could fate possibly spare them again?

Tanya knew she needed to leave the office for lunch despite the fact that she wasn't hungry. She drove south on I-75 and took M-59 towards Pontiac. While she had heard the stories, it was ironic that she felt deflated as she peered at the deflated roof of the Pontiac Silverdome. As the roof was starting to cave in for Chrysler executives, it had already caved for what once the crown jewel of sporting venues. She continued driving aimlessly through downtown Pontiac attempting to discern between irrational fear and the writing on the wall.

"No way would they lead into the Auto Show with an announcement of layoffs. That's just bad business," she thought to console herself.

The North American Auto Show is comparable to the Academy Awards for carmakers. Every year, thousands of car enthusiasts and plain ole folk who want a car to get them from A to B, converge onto downtown Detroit to "Ooh" and "Aah" at the auto industry's latest mechanical marvels. Each year, the two-week long showcase is prefaced with an expensive black-tie affair. For the black-tie affair, patrons pay exuberant prices for tickets with monies donated to charity. The night is a veritable Who's Who in the auto industry and metropolitan Detroit. Tanya had already purchased three sequined dresses with splits that tease and materials that accentuate her curves. She loved each of the dresses and would choose which based upon how it would coordinate with Oscar's tuxedo accessories.

The charity gala was Friday. "No way would they layoff before then," she thought with hollow self-assurance. "No way."

CHAPTER THIRTY-EIGHT

WEDNESDAY NIGHT

"Somebody need to get that big-legged girl a record deal!" Steve announced before adding, "Plus she finer than most of them plastic broads that be in the videos."

"She is a finer than silk thread," Wes added after a sip of beer. "You think Stokes hit it?"

Steve pondered a moment, "Yeah." He sipped his beer. "He gets real secretive about the ones he really likes. He only talks shit about unobtainable chicks on TV and stuff."

"Here comes Mr. Secrets now!" Wes announced

"Man, I know this sounds all sensitive and shit, but you glowing, pimp. You hit the lottery man?" Steve asked.

Wes joked, "He ain't carrying that guilty conscious about shacking with a married chick. What you see is relief then there's ole girl with them legs, up there with the band ..." Wes and Steve howled.

"Y'all fooling. I started a new consultant gig. It's part-time now, but it's giving me a chance to tap into my creative juices. Something I haven't done in a minute."

"Did you quit teaching?"

"Nah, still swinging that. Can't cut off my fa'sho' money before I get some mo' money!"

They all agreed in laughter.

The waitress came over and wrapped her arm around Stokely's waist. Radiating captivating perfume, she smiled at Stokely and then greeted all of them, "Ain't y'all missing somebody tonight?"

They looked at each other amusingly before Steve answered, "We saw Terrance on Friday and to see him again this soon would be out of character."

Wes added, "If he shows tonight, something must really be wrong."

Stokely was blushing as she continued to keep her arm around his waist longer than he was comfortable with. But then again, she knew how to work the guys for tips and in his mind Stokely had already decided that $5.00 of the $20.00 he planned to spend was for her tip.

"Let me see," the waitress said as she removed her arm from around Stokely and pointed at Steve. "You want another MGD" then she pointed at Wes, "You want another Heineken." When she turned to face Stokely, she placed her palm on his chest, "And I take it you want a Guinness except we're out tonight. Can you think of anything else you would like?"

Her smile and eyes were inviting. Stokely figured she might get a $7.00 tip from him tonight. He resisted the urge to say, "YOU!" and instead said, "I don't believe you. I bet y'all got some in the back."

Her smile was coy, "For you, I'll go check."

Then she pranced away with a little extra *umph* in the swinging of her hips. All six of their eyes were locked-in. Small beads of perspiration formed on Steve's forehead while Wes shook his head with a smile. Stokely was biting his lip when his phone buzzed from an incoming text. His face brightened when he saw it was from Phoenix.

Phoenix: Stokely?

He disregarded the unspoken *I'm-not-impressed-because-I'm-too-cool* delay that some people invoke when they receive a text. He typed back immediately.

Stokely: Hey Phoenix!! What's up?

Phoenix: Are you with your friends at Floods?

Stokely: Just got in.

Phoenix: Is Regina singing tonight?

Stokely: I think the band is in between sets. I haven't seen her yet.

Phoenix: When you see her, can you tell her I said that I'm going to come hear her soon.

Steve interjected, "Why won't you just call her? Shit all that thumb action is unnecessary. It's a phone, right?"

Stokely continued after giving Steve the side-eye. Wes was shaking his head indifferently. For the waitress, his head shaking was of reverence and appreciation. The head shake he had for Stokely was probably accompanied by thoughts that Stokely had fallen in love again.

Stokely: Sure can. How are you?

Phoenix: The new contract I was pursuing fell flat.

Stokely: Sorry about that. You know I was thinking about you and BBD. Have you ever considered a summer camp / program or something like that?

As evidence that he was out of his league when it comes to texting, Phoenix rattled off a flurry of rapid fire texts that had Stokely startled at the succession of buzzes.

Phoenix: OMG!!!

Phoenix: You are so smart!

Phoenix: I probably could get parents to pay and not have to hunt down a grant.

Phoenix: Where do you think I should host it?

Phoenix: We must get the cutest t-shirts!!!! I need my girls to stand out!

Phoenix: Stokely, THANK YOU!!!

Phoenix: You made my day!! XOXOXOXO

Phoenix: Have fun!!

Phoenix: Don't forget to tell Regina I said "Hi!"

Phoenix: Call me when you leave. I want to talk some more about your idea.

Phoenix: Ok, this is my last text. Call ME!

"Damn man, what did you do?" Wes asked.

Stokely was opening his mouth to explain when the waitress appeared with their drinks. Stokely had outstretched his arms as if to say, 'I don't know' when the waitress dipped under his arm and stepped between him in the table. As if her perfume wasn't enough, she set the tray on the table, rose to her tip toes, bent over the table while reaching to hand Steve his beer. Her bottom was less than an inch from the zipper on Stokely's pants.

Stokely's face exploded in worrisome delight. He was just thinking about Phoenix and was apprehended by this jiggly-assed waitress.

She stood back down to a flat-footed position and then back up to her tiptoes as she reached to hand Wes his Heineken. Stokely was transfixed at the jiggles beneath her skirt.

"How did you know that we had one special for you in the back?" she said as she turned to face him.

Stokely was speechless so he just smiled his best self-assured smile. She placed her hand on his chest again, "What else do you know?"

She let the hand linger.

All Wes and Steve needed was a bump and they would have burst into laughter, but they were trying to hold it in so Stokely wouldn't be further embarrassed.

"I know you gonna get a big tip."

"How big?"

There was a tingling arousal below his belt.

She patted his chest before turning to Wes and Steve. Her turn permitted her behind to breeze by Stokely's crouch. "Let me know when y'all ready to order some food." Then she turned back to Stokely, "Because I don't want you to be hungry." This time, the pat turned into a brief rub of his stomach before she walked away.

Their eyes followed as if magnetized.

"You can close your mouth now dawg," Wes chuckled.

"Man, sit your ass down before ole girl from the band see you seducing the help," Steve declared before taking a swallow of Miller Genuine Draft.

The band had already resumed their set but because he had been so distracted by the waitress, Stokely hadn't paid attention. As he began to take a seat, he focused on Gina's melodic re-interpretation of Eric Robeson's *Shake Her Hand*. To which during the hook about what the wise man once said, Wes and Steve sang along.

As he finally took his seat, Stokely shared, "I didn't tell y'all man. I've met someone. She's really special."

Wes and Steve looked at each other incredulously. As a testimony to their friendship, their thoughts were identical, "You mean someone that ain't the waitress or the singer?" But to give him a chance to speak, they both took a sip of their beer.

After exchanging puzzled glances, Steve broke the ice, "Not ole girl in the band? Someone else?"

Stokely, oblivious to his friend's surprise, "Yeah, man. Phoenix - she's cooler than a fan."

Steve and Wes both took long sips from their beers. Stokely knew he had some explaining to do.

CHAPTER THIRTY-NINE

THURSDAY MORNING

At 4:27 am, she was satisfied. Phoenix stepped back from the sprawl of scribblings, notes, and other remnants of her creative outburst that were spread over her loft's kitchen countertop island. Thankfully, Stokely was asleep. He called at 10:30 asking to come by. When he arrived, he witnessed how she had already drafted some logos and asked which of the program names he liked of the ten she created. He took the cue to begin browsing her records and books while leaving her to the flurry of activity.

After midnight, when she served him a coffee with a heavy dose of Bailey's, he had fallen asleep on the couch. Phoenix's coffee lacked Bailey's but had enough caffeine to fuel her energy for another couple of hours.

The summer program idea was a jewel. Her creativity had pushed her towards making it a photography camp where the girls would take pictures of sites around the city. Stokely had previously mentioned balancing the pictures of ruins along with pictures of still functioning beautiful structures. Once all the ideas coalesced in her mind, she became a creative force on steroids. Thankfully, she owns her own company and sets her own hours so she didn't have to worry about being in the office by 8:00 am.

Stokely was snoring. Maybe the Bailey's was too much, she hadn't considered how many drinks he may have had at Flood's. Nevertheless, the moment sort of resonated with her - to her right were remnants of her creativity that will become work that uplifts others and to her left was her man, who supported her dreams, resting comfortably in her home.

She made some chamomile tea and sat at the island taking in the moment. It was peaceful and serene. At five minutes to five am, she pulled the comforter from her bed and joined Stokely on the sofa. When she settled, he spoke a soft, "Hey baby" and kissed her on the forehead.

LEAVING Phoenix on the sofa was hard; yet by 8:30 am he was driving over to the abandoned train tracks. Phoenix's creativity was contagious and he was going to channel it through his first draft of renderings. He pulled out his camera and began taking a series of photos. He planned to make poster sized montages to reproduce the view in his office.

Three hours later after a quick shower and a bowl of cereal in his apartment, he was exiting the Renaissance Center copying store where he had developed 20 of the shots into large posters. Once he arrived in the office, he arranged them in order and began staring at them as if seeing something beyond the debris. He was talking to the pictures and himself when Edna interrupted.

"Mr. Robeson, how are you this morning?"

"Oh! hey! Ms. Ms.?"

"Pace."

"Like Judy Pace?" Stokely's dad's admiration of the actress used to prompt a playful jealously from his mother. To Cleve, Judy Pace was the bar against which beauty should be measured. He would have been proud to know his son took lessons to heart

Edna replied, "Yes, but much better."

They shared a smile. Edna surprised that a man Stokely's age knew Judy Pace and Stokely imaging how he would explain a woman better than Judy Pace to his dad.

Edna broke the silence with, "One of our partners will be out of town this weekend so we have extra tickets to the Auto Show Charity Gala on Friday. Would you like to come?"

Stokely was thinking that Edna was a world-class seductress. The way she batted her eyes and purred, "Would you like to come?" sent shivers throughout his imagination. He knew he was out of his league. He figured she been running game decades before he was born. He kept it civil and asked, "Can I have two tickets? I'd like to bring my girlfriend."

"Sure! That's no problem. Is she pretty?"

She said this with her hand on his bare forearm.

With a big prideful smile, he replied "The most beautiful woman since my mom."

Edna patted him on the cheek, "I knew you were a mama's boy!"

As she walked towards the door with that runway strut of hers, she said, "I'll hold the tickets for you upfront. Don't work too hard back here by yourself."

He wondered if her flirtatiousness was sincere or was she the type of woman who likes to know she can trigger a response from a man. He had the impression that she delights in the attention. He admitted she was a delightful sight, especially considering that he had her pegged between 65 -70 years old. He also figured that he would hold a spot for her in his vintage eye-candy category. But within seconds, his focus went back to the posters.

In his own way, he was replicating the creative energy demonstrated by Phoenix just hours before. He spent the next few hours researching the latest fitness parks and programs around the country. Years ago, Baltimore's Camden Yards set the tone for how downtown sports stadiums would be built in subsequent years; Stokely was searching for a fitness walkway precedent.

Around 2:15 pm, he received a text from Phoenix.

Phoenix: Hungry?

Stokely: For food or for you?

Phoenix: Food :-)

Stokely: When and where?

Phoenix: Have you had lunch?

Stokely: Not yet.

Phoenix: Meet me at my place in 30 minutes.

Stokely: I'll be there.

She met him at the door with a passionate welcoming kiss. With their tongues doing a tango to their own sensuous rhythm, Stokely lifted her from the floor and she wrapped her legs around his waist. Seconds later, with one arm wrapped around his neck and the other elbow on his shoulder with her fingers scrunching through Stokely's short cropped hair, Phoenix said, "I thought about you today."

Stokely was totally smitten. "I thought about you too Sunshine."

Phoenix smiled, "Sunshine?"

"Yeah, you brighten my day."

"Stokely Robeson, you are too much. Sunshine? How you gonna be cute and corny at the same time?"

She hopped down and beckoned him over to the kitchen island.

She had on sweats with no underwear or that was the impression given by the faint giggling of her rear end. "Had to be no underwear, who wears thongs when their home alone?" he thought. She had on an old t-shirt that appears to have been worn at some time when she was painting. The shirt had a small knot tied in the back and on the front, it read: I'M NOT SHORT; I'M FUN-SIZED! Her breast pressed against the cotton that signaled the absence of a bra. Her twists were pulled back into a twisty ponytail and her face was clear of make-up. Not that she wore much make-up, but the freshness of her skin made him think of the ladies in the Dove soap commercials.

There were two places set on the corner of the countertop island. Both plates held a tuna melt sandwich accompanied with kettle chips. Besides the plates were glasses of pome-granate juice and a smaller plate that held small salads with grape sized tomatoes. Phoenix picked one of the tomatoes and bit half and then offered the other half to Stokely.

"Like tomatoes?"

His gaze said, "I love you, I love you, I love you" but after taking the bite, his lips said, "Love 'em."

She gestured for his coat and as he was taking it off, he reached in the inside pocket and fetched tickets to the Auto Show Charity Gala. He waved them as if they were lottery tickets.

In a faux-European voice, Stokely bowed and asked, "Could I be so privileged to be accompanied to the most marvelous charity event by the most beautiful mademoiselle?"

She played along. Extending a limp hand and feigning surprise, "Oh my dearest lord, why I would be most obliged to accompany you for such a grand occasion."

Then with the suddenness of a light switch she said, "What am I going to wear?" Fret intruded her thoughts.

Stokely said, "If you wore what you have on now, you'd steal the show."

"Oh stop. You're trying too hard now," she said with a laugh.

As they sat at the island, she bowed her head for a second or two of grace, before asking, "What other wonderful things happened to you today?"

"Waking up to you was the highlight until you kissed me a few minutes ago."

Phoenix blushed.

"I tried to be creative like you were last night. I'm still in the minor leagues, but I got my juices flowing with ideas for my first renderings."

"How so?"

"I went by the tracks after I left and took goo-goobs of pictures. Then I got bunch of them blown-up to poster size. I have them lined around my work room at the MRO and I kind of talked to them so they could talk back, you know?" he said before taking a bite of his sandwich.

"You talk to photographs?" she asked sarcastically. "Is there anything else I should know? Wait. As a matter of fact, you haven't told me your story!"

Stokely looked at his watch as he finished chewing. "Well, I have a class soon so what if I told you I was 'boooooooooooorn,'" then extended his arms wide. Phoenix was non-plussed. "You better not say by no river, unless you're referring to Grand River Ave."

They both buckled over in laughter.

"How did you know I was going to go there?"

"Stokely, honey, you have a song for everything. Seriously, now. What else should I know in addition to your penchant for talking to photographs?"

"What if we do this - can you ask me a specific question and then I give you a specific answer?"

"Ooohhhh Stokely. Alright." Phoenix began a bit incredulously. "When were you born?"

"1978."

"Where were you born?"

"In a little ..." he then brought his fingers together like a steeple.

"No tent Stokely! For real!"

"Here in Detroit."

"This Q& A is boring."

"You're the one asking the questions," he took another bite of the tuna melt.

"Have you ever had your heart broken?"

He chewed slowly. "If I include Joi from the young people's choir, will that count?"

"How hard were you loving girls when you were in the young people's choir?"

"Joi kissed me once and asked would I sing for her. I had a reputation for lip-syncing in the choir stand. But that day, I was JAMMING!"

"So, Joi broke your heart?"

"Hell yeah. She didn't kiss me any of the other times the choir sang. Maybe she thought once was enough," Stokely looked around with a mock pensiveness.

Phoenix looked at him with an arched eyebrow. "Ok, okay, besides Joi. Seriously."

He met her gaze before sighing, "Steph. When I lived in DC, I had a girlfriend named Stephanie. I wouldn't say she broke my heart as much as I would say that my shortcomings in our relationship pushed her away and that broke my heart."

Phoenix nodded as she chewed as if to say, "Go on."

"I'll keep it simple. She was a sculptor and I was an architect - seems like a match made in heaven, right?" He took a small sip of juice before continuing, "Well, I was so consumed in being a successful architect I was putting in ridiculous hours. The first time it was an issue was when she had tickets for us to see the Margaret Garner Opera. I didn't even leave the office until after curtain rose. She was furious. I was immature, very immature. I thought success on the job equaled success in the relationship. Anyway, long story short, she told me that I acted as if she was 'Inconsequential.' Adding that it seemed like I'd be happy without her and she wanted me to be happy, so she left."

Phoenix stared at him for a while before asking, "Where is Steph now?"

"Married and living in Philadelphia."

"And you know this how?"

"Facebook."

"Do you miss her?"

Stokely was beginning to get bothered. "Nope."

"Why not?"

"I appreciate what I learned. I mean it hurt like hell when she left but had I not learned from that experience, I wouldn't be enjoying a wonderful lunch with you."

Phoenix shifted the direction of the conversation. "I'm excited about tomorrow."

Stokely relaxed, "Me too."

"Do you want me to drive?"

"Your Jeep?!"

"Nah man, my snowmobile. Yeah, my Jeep! Are you hating on BB?"

"BB?"

"Banana Bop, My Jeep's name!"

Stokely laughed heartily. "We can give Banana Bop the night off. I'll be by at 8."

CHAPTER FORTY

FRIDAY MORNING

Usually on the morning of the Charity Gala, Tanya is giddy with excitement but not this time. Punctuality is one of her many qualities, but this morning she lingered at her small table for two which was going to make her late. While at the table, she alternated between staring through the table's glass top and out the patio window with the thought of going to the office tormenting her.

Like thousands of blue and white-collar workers who have come before her, Tanya pondered exactly when she began to believe in the sincerity or better yet the concern for employees held by any of the Big Three automakers. History shows that in every moment of fiscal crisis, the employees suffer while the senior executives and stockholders endure minor inconveniences. The employees endure financial amputations and sometimes death but the big shots experience scratches or minor pulls.

She stared at her outstanding designer award from Chrysler. But countered the personal pride she felt for that achievement with the very real reality that the company abandoned the city of Highland Park and that city has been plummeting down an arson filled reality of despair ever since. If a company can abandon a city, it surely will discard employees. The pursuit and preservation of profits takes precedent over human beings, families, and communities.

But lingering beneath the surface of her doubts about the company's care for its employees were the nagging reminders that she had once again let things define her. The shortsighted belief that being essentially a high ranking middle manager made her 'Somebody' was a thought she tried to ignore. But instead, she could hear her mother telling her that, "Stuff out there doesn't make one happy in here" as she pointed to her heart. At one time, working on a doctorate was 'Stuff out there' until she finished the research and realized how much the process grew her. Then again, initially, Oscar was 'Stuff out there' but she matured and loved him for the supportive man he was. So now, as she peered over to the mirror on the wall, she had to be honest with herself. Chrysler should not dictate her life, she should. Worrying about layoffs won't prevent them from happening; in fact, worrying about them only exacerbates fear and obscures the fact that whatever happens it's all in God's divine plan.

With that, she began to get ready for the office determined to let the happiness in heart extend to influence the stuff out there. As she stood, she reached for her phone to check the voice message from the call she ignored while enraptured in her thoughts. It was Oscar.

"Good morning! I have my silver vest and tie to go with my tux. My flight leaves Nashville at 1pm. That should put me at your new place between 5 and 6. I can't wait to see how beautiful you'll look this evening."

Yep, 'Stuff out there' can be transformed into happiness in

here if we change our perspective, she thought as she began getting dressed.

～

TANYA WASN'T ALONE with renewed optimism. Phoenix's optimism was on a continuous upswing after arriving at Cleage Academy and being greeted by Starkiesha. Then she received an email from Mrs. Chisholm inviting her to speak with the Shuttlesworth PTA.

"Girl, let some of that rub off on me!" Regina greeted as she approached Phoenix, who smiled in response.

"Does Professor Robeson have something to do with your smile this morning?"

Phoenix held her hand up to show a pinching gesture.

"Oh, bullshit Phoenix!" They fell into an embrace laughing aloud.

"We're going to the Auto Show Charity Gala tonight," Phoenix said more excitedly than she wanted to reveal.

"Do you have something extra special to wear? I don't think they will let you in with crochet and denim," Regina joked.

"I know right. My mother made me buy a dress when we went to New York to catch the Motown Broadway show, I think I'll wear it."

"The black one you showed me a picture of with the back out?"

"Do you think it's okay?"

"Girl, you're liable to be the best dressed one there!" Regina exclaimed and then added, "You need to let me do your makeup. What time should I come by?"

"You don't think I can do my own makeup?"

"Phoenix, who did your makeup last time you wore that dress?"

"My mom," she responded bashfully. "Point taken. Can you be there by 6:30?"

They laughed as Regina replied, "I got you girl."

ELAINE WAS SURPRISED to see her baby boy. His arrival broke the monotonous repetition of retirement. She found retirement to be overrated. Besides not having to be somewhere at a designated time, the daily routine was boring her. She had only been retired four months and knew she needed do something to break this routine. Cleve maintained a steady schedule of plumbing jobs which took him out of the house following their daily breakfast. But even breakfast was becoming routine as Cleve would cook and she would clean once they ate and he left. Yoga was ok and book clubs were cool, but what Elaine really wanted was to take a road trip through the 48 continental states. She couldn't figure how she would convince Cleve to drive to Alaska, but maybe a cruise there once they got to Washington would be fun.

She was browsing vacation sites on the internet when she heard Stokely's key in the door. Seconds later, the timbre of her son's voice brightened her morning.

"Hey Ma! How's it going this morning?" he said extending his arms for a hug.

"Not too bad for an old country girl from Arkansas," she replied as they embraced. She then took one of Stokely's hands in hers and peered at it inquisitively while massaging each finger. She then added, "It doesn't seem as if any of your fingers are broken." She repeated the treatment with his other hand, "These fingers seem alright too." She then turned the guilt trip on full blast, "So I can't seem to figure out why these fingers can't punch a few numbers on the telephone so somebody could see how their mother is doing?"

Stokely had no answer besides a boyish blush.

"Well, well! This new little lady must be special to make a man neglect his Mama," Elaine added playfully. "Why don't you sit down and tell me all about her? Didn't you say her name was Phoenicia or something?"

"Ma! Phoenix!" He said laughing. "Phoenicia, Ma? You know you made that up!"

"You know everybody thought me and Cleve had lost our marbles when we named you and your sister. We wanted to show our cultural heritage, but these folks nowadays just name the kids any ole' thang. Some of these kids are named after alcoholic drinks!" Elaine said incredulously. "Makes one long for the days of Shirley, Barbara, or Cletus. Well, maybe not Cletus, but you know what I mean."

"I met a guy named Zaire the other day."

"See his mama almost had it. She was thinking culturally but Zaire is what the exploiters named the land. Although I doubt she would have to preferred to name her child Congo. But anyway, that ain't what you came here for. When are you going to let me and Cleve meet Miss Phoenix? You ain't shamed of her looks, are you?"

"Oh Ma!"

"Don't 'Oh Ma' me! Cleve and I prayed day and night for you when you went through that lost puppy stage dating all them homely looking girls." Elaine teased before adding, "She ain't married, is she?"

"She is not married. Plus, the next time, I'm with a married woman she's going to be married to me!"

"Boy, you say that with the conviction of born again Christian. But I'd rather not hear what you claiming to never do cause that ain't worth a hill of beans. Tell me about Phoenix. You got any pictures?"

Stokely showed Elaine the picture Phoenix sent him a few days ago.

"Oh, she is pretty. She got some innocent eyes. I love her hair! Stokely how old is she? She doesn't look a day past 22." Elaine said while continuing to hold the phone analyzing Phoenix's picture.

"She's 27."

"She's a keeper Stokely. It's in the eyes. Plus, you say she does community work with kids? You know I respect a woman who is committed to the community. Everybody talking about how bad the city is while they twiddling their thumbs waiting on somebody else to make a difference, this girl is doing something. I like her. When are you going to bring her by?"

"What about Sunday? After church?"

"You are serious! She got you to go to church?"

Stokely could only laugh because he knew whatever he said would be used against him in his mother's court of rationale.

"Ok, I'll leave you alone about Miss Phoenix. How's the new job?" was Elaine' segue into another conversation. She asked while heading to the coffee pot. It isn't every day that a man can enjoy a midday cup of coffee with his mother. But as far as Stokely could see this was the beginning of what promises to be a wonderful day.

CHAPTER FORTY-ONE

EARLY FRIDAY EVENING

Regina and Phoenix were giggling like schoolgirls when Stokely rang the buzzer. Stokely had seen Regina's car in the visitor's parking spot and spent the last few minutes calming himself. The situation between him and Gina occurred so close to the start of his relationship with Phoenix. Technically or perhaps with man logic, he should be worry-free. Yet; he sensed a vulnerability and an overprotectiveness in Phoenix that at best may cause her to overreact once she found out. He knew the longer he went without saying anything the more likely it would be a disruptive matter. She would figure that he was hiding something else and then the avalanche of projected issues that stem from the "What else are you hiding?" question would smother their relationship's potential. Talking to Phoenix about Regina would be a tough conversation. One that he would not initiate, at least not tonight.

When the door opened, he was thunderstruck like the first time he saw the full-page photo of Dawn from En Vogue featured in *Vibe Magazine*. Regina opened the door. He chose to ignore the symbolism of her standing between him and Phoenix. He figured she was dressed to perform tonight at Flood's. It wasn't fair that she opened the door then turned and bent over to pick up some type of bag. The patterns on her leggings were hypnotizing. To not look at her butt was like defying gravity, there was a slight strain in his neck to keep from looking.

He was rewarded for his effort as Phoenix was standing straight ahead looking like a regal goddess. By wearing her hair in an up-do, her cheekbones were accentuated and the dimples that accompanied her smile were a knockout punch. Stokely gasped. "My god ..."

"My girl is looking good ain't she?" Regina added with pride.

Stokely was working to catch his breath as he stood with his mouth agape. He nodded in agreement. To hell with being cool, he wanted to bask in splendor of Phoenix

He estimated the height of her heels as she was considerably taller but not quite 5'4". However, the dress and how it pronounced her curves demanded the bulk of his attention. Later that night, as he admired her bare back, he would ponder bra technology because her breasts were on magnificent display. Given her stature, her breasts were a wonderful compliment to her dimensions, but in this dress, they had a full perkiness he hadn't noticed before. He always believed the inventors of the push-up bra deserved their own holiday but that wouldn't explain how enticing Phoenix's breasts were tonight. Then again, the tear shaped opening that starts at the dress' collar and provides a teasing peek at her cleavage may be the culprit.

"Y'all have a good time! And Professor Robeson, be sure to bring Phoenix to Flood's sometimes! Bye!" The door closing behind him snapped Stokely out of his trance.

"Baby, you look absolutely stunning. I knew you were fine, but gotdamn baby!"

Stokely didn't have the fashion vocabulary to name the material that made Phoenix's dress have an iridescent shimmer in the light, but the black and silver material served as an exclamation mark punctuating Phoenix's beauty.

"Thanks, Stokely. By the way, you're wearing that tuxedo! Can we promise to make going somewhere nice a priority in our relationship?"

Stokely extended his right pinky finger and said, "I pinky swear."

When they hooked pinkies, he pulled her close. He went to kiss her but she moved her head, "I can't mess up my makeup baby. I just got it done." They chuckled together.

HE TIMED IT PERFECTLY. From how long it would take for her to style her dreads to how many times she would change either dresses, stockings, make-up, or shoes - Oscar knew his wife. Or at least tonight's experience was an early step toward reaffirming what he thought he knew about his wife.

A full minute hadn't passed from the time Tanya emerged from the bedroom modeling her dress until the town car called to say it was outside. To maximize the time with his wife, Oscar arranged for them to be chauffeured to the gala. Minutes later, as he sat in the rear seat of the luxury sedan with Tanya holding his arm, not only did he feel like being chauffeured was excellent idea, he also could feel the scotch tape being applied to the cracks in his heart regarding his wife's affair. He was healing and that made him happy.

AS THEY PROCEEDED south on Woodward Ave. toward downtown, Phoenix reflected on how wonderfully things had been going with Stokely. Was this really happening? Could she be falling in love? Besides being fresh out of a live-in relationship and punching Pedro, Stokely has been wonderful. She really couldn't believe she was in a dating relationship with the potential become more serious. She was watching as he drove while rapping along with the music. To her, he is one surprise after another. She hadn't felt like this in years and they haven't been together a week. Even in admiration, she could feel her heart tapping on the safety brake - ready to stop the wheels of emotion from turning should one of his surprises be something too surprising to bear.

CHAPTER FORTY-TWO

FRIDAY EVENING

After making it through valet parking and coat check, Stokely and Phoenix were overflowing with excitement. The combination of the fairytale beginning of their relationship, their pride in how well the other was looking, and the overall festive climate of the event was an intoxicating mix that had them floating though the convention floor.

"Which cars do you want to check out first?" Phoenix asked.

"I heard they may have a big bodied Cadillac concept car that I want to see. I also want to see if Lincoln is going to step their game up. I kinda want to check out all of them, well most of them. I don't really do foreign cars."

"You don't do foreign cars? What's up with that?"

"C'mon Sunshine. Look at our city or even the national economy - if we are spending or sending our money over to Japan or Germany, what's going to happen to jobs over here?"

"Yeah baby, I hear you. But there is something to be said for trade-in value and minimal repairs." She allowed the idea to take root before saying, "Look! That's the cutest little thing!" as she pointed at the small sized Lincoln SUV.

She took as big of strides as her legs and that dress would permit and with a short hop she was into the driver seat. She ran her hand along the dash and the elbow rest compartment. She turned to Stokely and posed.

"Can you see me in this?"

Stokely laughed, "I sure can!"

Phoenix flipped the sun visor down and checked her makeup in the mirror. She turned her head from side to side as if checking her earrings.

Stokely inserted, "You know if the mirror situation ain't right, we're going to leave that car with the dealer."

Phoenix rolled her eyes playfully before beckoning Stokely to come sit in the passenger seat. As he was sitting, she said, "I love these panoramic sunroofs. If I had to get rid of Banana Bop, my next car has to have one of these." They both peered upward as if they could see the skies instead of the dark ceiling of Cobo Arena.

"I HATE TO SAY IT, but these Cadillacs are beautiful!" said Tanya as she ran her hand along the roofline of the Cadillac XTS.

Oscar joked, "I'll keep a lookout to make sure none the Chrysler executives see you admiring the competition." To which Tanya looked both ways before ducking into the driver seat.

Unlike others, her admiration for the interior was not the admiration of a consumer but of a fellow artist. She was taking design cues that maybe she could incorporate into some future Chrysler designs. She touched every button, opened every compartment, and even closed the door to measure the space from the dashboard to the panel of the door. With photographic memory, she noted the stitching of the leather and the sight lines from the rearview mirror through the slanted rear window.

Oscar could only smile. She was more of an auto design enthusiast than he would ever be. He tapped on the window to get her attention. She held up one finger with her left hand while her body was turned and she was using the distance from the tip of her thumb to the tip of her pinky to approximate how high the rear seat sat from the floor.

She was nodding her head as if impressed. Once she got out the car, she faced Oscar as if talking to him but she was really thinking aloud. "They made a mistake by promoting this as the replacement for the DTS. They should have just introduced it as a new vehicle and kept the DTS. This thing doesn't have the dimensions and I hear it's powertrain is underwhelming. Plus, it's shackled down by the expectations of a dedicated consumer base that likes the large sedan."

Oscar nodded in agreement. There wasn't much he could add. He imagined she feels the way he feels now when he is explaining how although he loves Miles Davis' *Bitches' Brew* and *In a Silent Way*, maybe the artistic step towards electronic instruments was the beginning of the end traditional jazz bands. Tanya would listen to him with a minimal interest in the subject while respecting his interest in such a matter. When it came to cars, Tanya critiqued them with a discernment that normal human beings would never be able to muster.

"I don't want to be over in the General Motors section too long, are there any other cars that you would like to see?"

Oscar replied, "It's been years since I've had a Corvette, let's head over to the Chevy section and see the new Corvettes."

"YOU LIKE TWO DOOR CARS HUNH?" Stokely teased. "What about the baby seat?"

"Excused me, Mr. Robeson. But I'm not thinking about baby seats until after I'm married."

"Then I guess Banana Bop is your last two door."

Phoenix stopped and smiled, "You ain't slick buddy. But you do know that conversation starts with a ring and proposal, right?"

"How you know I don't have a diamond on layaway right now!"

"You just don't stop with the charm, do you?" Phoenix replied playfully. "But seriously, you know how you feel about foreign cars?" Stokely nodded. "I feel that way about blood diamonds - no diamonds for me. Should we get to that point, let's ring shop together."

"That's cool, let's make it a plan. Well, if we must represent the two-door life, let's make sure we check out the new Vettes sometime tonight."

"Wow. I haven't been in one in a long time. My dad had one when I was a little bitty girl."

"You still little bitty!"

"Don't let little bitty knock you out!" Phoenix said while playfully waving her fist.

Stokely took her fist into his hands and worked his fingers around until their fingers were intertwined. He leaned in and kissed her on cheek. "I don't want a little bitty beat down, I just want you. C'mon let's look at your last two door car."

CHAPTER FORTY-THREE

FRIDAY EVENING

Stokely and Phoenix strolled through the charity gala holding hands like high school lovebirds with matching outfits on the school trip to the amusement park. They were so giddy with each other, callous-hearted people would be nauseous at the sight of their public displays of affection. When they saw a car with a lot of people waiting to sit inside, they engaged in face-to-face embraces while they awaited their turn. Quite simply, they were so enraptured with each other it as if they were the only ones at the gala.

OSCAR NOTED that there was a lengthy line to sit in the driver's seat of the Corvette, so he opted for the passenger side where the wait was shorter. As they waited, Tanya was critiquing the design. She was explaining how they preserved the integrity of the Corvette design while revising its overall look. Oscar stepped down into the passenger seat and a "Whoa" escaped him as he underestimated how low the car sat.

"Are you ok?" Tanya asked.

"Yes, yes, I'm fine. I just didn't realize it was so low," he chuckled.

The young lady in the driver seat smiled at him before flipping down the sun visor.

Outside of the car, Tanya had stopped admiring the design as she looked across the top of the car at Stokely. It wasn't anger. But something gave her pause as they looked at each other.

Stokely was extending his hand to Phoenix as he dryly greeted, "Hey Tanya."

Oscar missed the exchange. Besides being embarrassed about damn near falling into the car, he was a tad puzzled but didn't want to stare at the young lady. It seemed that she looked familiar. As she exited the car, he turned as to respectfully not look at her behind; yet, for a few seconds his mental rolodex was flipping furiously trying to place her. As he turned to step out, he heard Tanya say, "Hi Stokely. Are the two of you enjoying the evening?"

Phoenix had figured that she liked the Lincoln MKC the best so far because she preferred to sit higher up. She also was relieved to step out of the car because the old man next to her seemed to be staring. As she placed both feet on the carpet outside of the car, she grabbed Stokely's hand to pull herself up. While standing, she heard him say, "Hey Tanya."

This was it. The moment when she had to face Stokely's ex-girlfriend. She gave herself a quick mental overview. Her hair, her make-up, her dress, her shoes were all good. In her mind, she wanted to look her best when this moment arrived. It was petty, but she wanted the ex-girlfriend to know Stokely had moved on to better things.

While holding her hand, Stokely guided Phoenix around the front of the car. She noticed that the ex-girlfriend was very tall. She had to be over six feet. Oh God, did Stokely prefer tall women? This lady was gorgeous.

Tanya recognized Phoenix from Slow's. She also recognized that Stokely was completely taken by her. She was very pretty, almost girlish in appearance. Tanya knew that meeting this young lady was of minor consequence, she was more nervous about how Oscar would respond.

Oscar stepped from the Corvette still attempting to place the young lady's face. He had heard Tanya greet Stokely. When he stood, she had begun walking towards the front of the car. He saw Stokely and his heart dropped. Anger began to simmer. He noticed the young lady was with Stokely. This mellowed his anger a tad as he hoped the young lady was proof that Stokely had moved on and wasn't plotting a return. He followed Tanya. They all reached the front of the car at nearly the same time.

Stokely extended his hand first to Oscar. He then spoke to Tanya in a manner of introduction. "Mr. and Mrs. Rousseau, I would like to introduce you to my girlfriend, Phoenix Ellison." As he introduced, he looked toward Phoenix who seemed ashen. He continued the introductions, "Phoenix, meet Mr. and Mrs. Oscar Rousseau."

"Dad?"

Oscar stood rigidly as if frozen in ice.

Tanya was aghast.

Stokely was flummoxed.

Phoenix was dumbfounded.

While his heart was well-intended, Stokely couldn't find the words to continue the introductions. His hands were moving and his head swiveled, but no words escaped his throat.

"Dad?" Tanya asked. "Oscar, is this your daughter?"

Stokely and Tanya's eyes went back and forth between the pair. The faint freckles and the noses could have been corroborating evidence to their connection.

Phoenix's eyes never left Oscar. Closer inspection would note that her eyes were welling up with tears. A whole confluence of emotions avalanched through her spirit rendering her spooked in appearance and at an utter complete loss for words.

If the strong whir of airplane propellers could be captured in a vacuum tunnel, that would come close to the confused disorientation whirring through Oscar's mind.

His mind was not the only thing off to the races.

His heart rate catapulted and he began to gasp from a shortness of breath. It appeared that he was reaching for Phoenix or attempting to brace himself on the hood of the car. If he thought the Corvette's seats were low, then the attempt to balance himself on the hood proved that the front end of a Corvette sat even lower.

Oscar fell to the ground.

"MR. ROUSSEAU!" Stokely shouted.

"OSCAR!" Tanya screamed.

Phoenix watched as though she were in an alternate universe or seeing the situation as an event on television.

Oscar's face was turning from red to maroon as Stokely rolled him over to his back. Without hesitation, Stokely began to administer CPR. Tanya kneeled behind him crying with worry. Phoenix was paralyzed with emotion, looking down with both palms upward as if frozen in thought. A crowd began to gather. Another patron dialed 911. One patron began recording the situation with his smartphone.

To Oscar, all sound faded and the commotion seem to be in slow-motion. His chest felt as if the Incredible Hulk had bound all of Oscar's nerves into a tightly clenched fist, twisted the fist, and began tugging them through his chest. It even hurt to breathe. He couldn't remember why he did not like Stokely. But he felt gratitude that Stokely was breathing for him. The facial winces Stokely saw on Oscar's face were rooted both in Oscar's pain and from a deep desire to say thank you. But the words simply could not come out.

Stokely was surgically mechanic in his administration of CPR. With every wince of Oscar's face, he was further charged in his effort to save Oscar's life. Given Stokely's spirit, he probably would have administered CPR to anyone in need, but this CPR session had purpose - purpose for Tanya and purpose for Phoenix.

By the tenth rotation of chest pumps and breathing into Oscar's mouth, the on-site emergency team had made their way over. With a stretcher and defibrillator, they pushed back the small crowd and took over medical procedures.

Stokely fell back to a seat on his bottom and took some short scoots backward to give the team space to work. He could see Tanya crying and he could see the emergency team tearing away Oscar's shirt. What he did not see was Phoenix back away from the crowd.

CHAPTER FORTY-FOUR

LATER FRIDAY EVENING

A t first glance, when Stokely looked over his right shoulder and did not see Phoenix he assumed the crowd had converged in front of her. When he looked over his left shoulder, he calculated that from when he last saw her, she should have been over his right shoulder.

He looked again.

Then he looked floor level, figuring he could spot her pretty toes in those lovely heels among the legs and feet of the crowd. But he didn't see them.

He heard Oscar coughing and intuitively sensed a decreasing of panic in the crowd. Yet, while it seemed as if the crowd began to gather some assurance that Oscar would not die in the middle of the floor, Stokely began to panic.

He bolted to his feet.

"Phoenix?"

"Phoooee-nnixx?"

"Phoenix!"

"PHOENIX!!"

He was on his tip-toes looking over the heads of the gathered patrons. He then began to part to the crowd, frantically looking in every direction for where she might be or headed.

Did she disappear?

"PHOENIX!!!"

Where the hell did she go?

Is she okay?

"PHOENIX!!!"

"Maybe she sat down somewhere," he thought. Thinking that between seeing the father who had abandoned her, seeing Tanya, and knowing that her current boyfriend's ex-girlfriend was married to her father - Stokely figured all that was way too much at one time. With his head-on swivel in every direction, he retraced the steps they had taken since they arrived not knowing his effort would be futile.

BY THE TIME Stokely thought to retrace their steps, Phoenix was outside flagging a cab. She didn't bother to stop at coat check. With the barrage of emotions battering against the beaches of her mind like ocean waves in a typhoon, Phoenix was oblivious to her coat and the freezing temperatures outside. In a dress with the back out and shoes with the toes out, she rushed outside on a frigid January night in Detroit. She was in the back seat of a cab before her teeth would begin to chatter. "Take me to Burns Street in Indian Village!" she shouted before the cab driver could ask where she was headed.

The cab had made its way onto Jefferson Avenue traffic before Stokely rushed out the door looking bewildered. "Where the fuck did she go?" he kept repeating to himself to ignore the growing notion that she was gone. He was standing outside in the cold when he saw the ambulance pull away from Cobo Hall.

Even his wishes for Oscar's well-being did not diminish the fear the of Phoenix's disappearance.

He watched the ambulance lights head north on Washington before hanging a right on what he assumed was Fort Street. Something magnetic about the lights held his attention. Their brightness, flashing frequency and subsequent disappearance around the corner seemed an odd confirmation that Phoenix had left.

He stood for another few moments attempting to sort out what happened in the manner that someone would dump jigsaw pieces and begin using their hands to push the pieces around to try to conjure some type of pattern, some type of order, some type of sense.

"Oscar is her dad?"

"Damn."

CHAPTER FORTY-FIVE

LATE FRIDAY EVENING

Denise was enjoying a tall glass of gewürztraminer, her favorite winding-down beverage, when BooBaby began barking. The lights from a taxi cab shone through the large bay window and along the living room walls before alighting upon the garage door at the end of the driveway. With BooBaby by her side, Denise opened the door to witness Phoenix stepping from the rear seat.

Noticing that Phoenix didn't have on a coat sparked matriarchal concern within Denise. With her left hand clutching her robe closed, she opened the screen door with her right hand as Phoenix rushed through.

"What happened? Where is your coat? Don't you know it's Jan ..."?

Phoenix interrupted her, "I saw Oscar. My dad was there! It was terrible!"

Denise began to calm as she sensed nothing physically had happened to Phoenix, whose dress and hairstyle appeared neat. The only thing disheveled about her daughter was the makeup ruined by tears. Denise had hoped that by giving Phoenix Oscar's phone number that she would arrange to see her father on her own terms. Obviously, that isn't what happened tonight.

As she closed and locked the front door, Denise took off her robe and draped it around Phoenix's shoulders. "Baby, have a seat and I'll go get you some wine. Seeing your father couldn't have been that bad."

BooBaby nuzzled against Phoenix's thigh and seemed to guide her towards the sofa. Before sitting, Phoenix put her arms through the sleeves and tied the robe around her waist. When she sat, BooBaby sat on the floor close to her and laid her huge head in Phoenix's lap. As Phoenix began to pet BooBaby's head, Denise entered the room with a warm face cloth draped over her forearm and two glasses of wine.

In a moment of mother to daughter endearment, Denise sat the wine down and used the cloth to clear Phoenix's face of makeup. After some vigorous wiping, Denise stepped back to survey her work. Then it hit her, "Where's Stokely?"

The question brought a new wave of tears from Phoenix. Witnessing that, Denise left the room and returned with the whole bottle of gewürztraminer. She then finished her glass in one long gulp before sitting next to her daughter. She reached for the wash cloth again, folded it to the unstained side, and resumed wiping Phoenix's face.

"Phoenix. Honey, I'm confused what happened?"

Phoenix took a deep breath before sipping her wine. "Remember I told you Stokely just broke up with his girlfriend?"

"Yeah, I remember. But..." Denise's words trailed off as a new idea burst from her lips. "He didn't leave you at the Auto Show for that hussy, did he?"

"No," Phoenix said between sniffles. "She's married."

"Stokely's ex-girlfriend eloped after they broke up?"

"No mom. It's worse."

Denise poured herself some more wine. "Phoenix, you're not making any sense. And what does all this have to do with your father?"

BooBaby jumped into Phoenix's lap as if giving her a hug. Phoenix resumed petting her head while looking at her mother with a 'I-don't-want-to -say' expression.

"Did Stokely meet your father?"

Phoenix nodded 'yes' while adding, "Actually Stokely introduced me to him."

Denise was surprised. "He already knew Oscar?"

"It seems that way. He said, 'this is Mr. and Mrs. Rousseau."

"Ooohhh, Oscar's wife was there. Is she pretty?"

"Very."

"So why did you bring up Stokely's ex-girlfriend? I don't get it."

Phoenix grimaced painfully.

"Was her husband there too?"

Phoenix grimaced a bit tighter this time.

"I'm not following you honey. So, you met your father and his wife and you ran into Stokely's ex-girlfriend, who is married, and her husband?"

"We met at the same time, mom."

"I bet that was awkward, all six of you being together at the same time. How did Stokely introduce his ex? Does her husband know about ... you know ... Stokely and the wife?"

"Mom, it was just four of us."

"Wait, I'm confused. Four?"

"Yes." Phoenix held up four fingers, "Four of us, mom - four."

BooBaby looked at Denise, then proceeded to lay at Phoenix's feet and use her paws to cover her face.

"Four? I'm confused. You." Denise extended one finger.

"Stokely." Two fingers.

"Oscar." Three fingers.

"His wife." Four fingers.

"Stokely's ex-girlfriend." Five fingers.

Phoenix shook her head in a vigorous 'no' motion.

"But that is five." Denise's brow furrowed. She took a long sip of wine. "Unless, you mean ..." she used her index finger in an arcing motion for emphasis. "Stokely's ex is ..." the finger went back to the original point as if she drew an imaginary protractor.

Phoenix nodded a slow 'yes.'

"His ex is Oscar's wife?"

Phoenix gave a slow affirming nod.

Denise finished her glass.

"Oh, my God." Denise grabbed the whole bottle of wine.

"Mom, please."

After a small sip, Denise placed the bottle down, waved her hands as if she were fanning herself, and exhaled a "Whew." She took a few short but exaggerated breaths before adding, "Well, I can understand that, that, that is a lot. I mean, WHEW Lord Jesus! How often does that happen? But why did you leave without your coat? Did you know his ex was married?"

"Yes mom, He told me before tonight. I figured we'd date some more before asking him how it came to be. But mom, that's not the worse."

Denise reached for her wine bottle again but Phoenix waved her off.

"I think Oscar had a stroke."

Denise's eyes expanded in horror. Then her eyes pleaded with Phoenix as they darted back and forth from the wine bottle back to Phoenix. Phoenix nodded.

"Stokely was giving him CPR when I just backed out of the

crowd and left. It was all just too much mom. Too much, too soon."

Sobs began to turn to tears while Denise came over from her chair and wrapped her arms around Phoenix. BooBaby sat up and nuzzled her nose in between them.

"Oh baby, baby, baby. It's going to be okay. You hear me? It's going to be okay."

Denise then commenced to humming and rocking Phoenix in her arms. "It will work itself out. You just watch. All of this ... it'll all work out."

CHAPTER FORTY-SIX

MUCH LATER FRIDAY EVENING

Stokely retrieved both of their coats from coat check. While waiting for valet, a couple pointed at Stokely and the husband gave him a thumbs up while the wife clapped and said, "You're a hero!"

Stokely smiled a painful, appreciative smile while hoping the valet would hurry. When the valet arrived, he asked, "Will the lady be joining you?" as he held the door for Stokely.

"Nah man. She had to leave."

"That wasn't her in the ambulance, was it?"

"Nah, it was her dad."

"I hope he pulls through and everything works out."

"I hope so too man. I hope so too."

Stokely tipped the valet and hopped into the driver seat. Once inside, he plugged in his iPod and selected shuffle. Whenever he was troubled, Stokely went on long drives through the city. Sometimes, he would take Grand River all the way from downtown to Seven Mile. Then take Seven Mile east towards Woodward Ave. and then take Woodward south back towards downtown. Tonight, he opted for the eastside route of a similar nature and took Gratiot away from downtown towards Seven Mile.

When the music began, the cabin of the F150 was filled with bluesy sounds of Bobby "Blue" Bland mournfully wailing about the members only private party.

At the stoplight, Stokely reached for Phoenix's coat and held it to his nose. He had been at fault in relationships before, but this time he couldn't bear to lose Phoenix over something that was beyond his control. Stokely had promised himself that he wouldn't allow his past to disrupt his future; yet, that was exactly what was happening.

"Damn."

CHAPTER FORTY-SEVEN

EARLY SATURDAY MORNING

There was a tug-of-war inside Tanya's soul. She had been contrite over the situation regarding Stokely; yet, she could now say she knew the bitter taste of resentment because she never knew Oscar had a daughter. In all their years of marriage, he never mentioned his child. His flippant disregard to having been previously married had been reduced to "We were young" and "annulment." Now she felt betrayed because he had withheld essential information and was further embittered at the thought of how long he would have kept the secret.

Her anger would have to wait. As she viewed Oscar sleeping with IVs and other tubes connected to him, her thoughts wandered to just a few days before when she was in the hospital and Oscar was sitting bedside. Sitting bedside in a chair that had just shortly before been occupied by Stokely.

Stokely.

The irony was that she had feared that Stokely would be the thing to drive her and Oscar apart and now he is the same thing reuniting Oscar with his daughter.

Tanya sat quietly as a few truths bubbled to the surface of her thinking.

If her marriage is going to work, Oscar is going to have to forgive her for her relationship with Stokely. And she is going to have to forgive Oscar for not telling her about his daughter.

As if those ideas had morphed into opposing ping pong players, the notion of forgiveness bounced side to side in her mind. With the scariest thought of an imaginary reconciliation when Oscar would invite his daughter to their home and she would bring her boyfriend. "Oh God!" thought Tanya. She wisely turned her attention to the moment, to the facts. Oscar was breathing. Stokely's CPR helped Oscar's recovery chances and possibly saved his life. Her other man had breathed new life into her marriage. She was going to need a drink after this.

CHAPTER FORTY-EIGHT

SATURDAY MORNING

C leve pushed open the unlocked door to Stokely's apartment. "This boy ain't packed shit," he thought. He surveyed the layout, then thought, "It ain't shit to pack really." Stokely had joked that he liked open spaces and the last few days have provided an opportunity to bask in the openness of this lonely apartment.

Cleve was too cool to panic, but the unlocked door brought some fears to mind. As he walked slowly through the apartment, it didn't appear that the place had been ransacked. Wouldn't be much to ransack anyhow. As he made it to the doorway of one of the bedrooms, he saw his son.

Faced down and spread eagle across a futon. He still had on his tux. Tucked under one arm was a woman's coat.

Cleve listened intently and could focus on Stokely's light and sporadic snore. "He's not dead, thank God," he thought as he approached his sleeping son.

He did the best he could to soften his baritone, reached for

Stokely's shoulder, and gave a slight push. "Son." He pushed again. "Stokely, c'mon son, wake up." The last push did the job.

Stokely stirred and turned to look in his father's face. "Oh shit, I forgot I was going to start moving today!" raced through his mind. With the mind-reading wisdom of a father, Cleve said, "Seems like you had quite a night to make you forget about moving, hunh?"

Stokely smiled and began to sit up.

Cleve added, "I'mma grab some drinks from your fridge. We gonna need to talk about why you all snuggly with the jacket instead of the woman."

As Cleve headed for the kitchen, Stokely retrieved three of the empty milk crates he was going to use to pack his music cds. By the time he picked them up, he heard his father say, "God-damn boy, you got this smoothie shit but didn't think to cop some beers. She done sho'nuff put it on ya'."

Stokely stacked two milk crates near the window with a view of Greektown and the other crate a few feet away - the circumstances were not so severe that they needed to be sitting right next to each other. This was not a time to break some man rules. Plus, Stokely figured after he told his father what happened, he will have broken enough other man rules to max out his cool man credit line.

Cleve handed Stokely the green smoothie while saying, "I'mma try this mango shit. I hear it puts more yen in your yang."

To the uninitiated, Cleve's language would sound abrasive. Yet, to hear Cleve speak, was to hear the love and admiration he held for his son draped all over his rough choice of words. Once when Stokely scored two points in a little league basketball game where his team scored forty, Cleve greeting Stokely afterwards with a headlock and the most endearing way one could say, "This my little motherfucker right here." Followed by a soft knuckle rub to the temple and a pat on the back. The moment eradicated the self-loathing Stokely felt for dribbling the ball off his foot and earning more fouls than points. From those memories and others, Stokely knew that Cleve's references to smoothies as shit was just his way of saying he was going to try something new while sounding supportive.

Cleve sat on the stacked crates and Stokely sat on the one. They both took sips of their smoothies while facing the window.

"You got all these at Whole Foods or something?"

Stokely nodded.

Cleve looked at the smoothie label, while commenting, "This look like some packaged juicer shit. But it don't taste half bad."

After another sip and another moment of silence, Cleve followed a long sigh with a rhetorical question, "So she left you, hunh?"

Stokely rather pitifully replied, "Which one?"

Cleve nodded slowly, "Yeah, you got a point there." He took another sip. "The new girl - Elaine said we was gonna meet her tomorrow. I guess we can ice that idea." He was looking at Stokely who was looking out the window.

Stokely meekly agreed, "Yeah, we gotta ice that."

"Look son," Cleve said tentatively in a hope to frame the conversation just so. "Sleeping with the coat? That's some new shit. I mean, I know you all gentlemanly and helped her out of coat and all. But damn, where'd she go?"

Stokely shook his head slowly, "I don't know. I wish I did."

Cleve surmised the situation. "Nah son, it's best you don't know."

"Hunh?"

"If you knew, you'd only try to make something happen when now maybe just ain't the time."

Stokely stirred and looked at his father.

"You got the coat, right?"

Stokely nodded.

"Well, shit. She'll be back. She gotta get her coat." He took another sip of the smoothie. "Yo' mama is gonna have a shit load of questions for me when I get home. So, tell me how you end up with the coat and no woman. That way yo' mama won't be pestering me for the details."

Stokely took a long sip and grimaced over the taste. Cleve added, "That's why I gave that green shit to you." Stokely chuckled before starting his story.

HE WAS NEARLY FINISHED RECOUNTING the experiences of the last few days when Cleve started smiling and humming.

Stokely pressed forward with his recap before Cleve interrupted him with his Otis Redding impersonation and singing about how young girls get weary.

"Dad, what are you talking about?"

"Nah, go on and finish your story, son."

Stokely resumed as Cleve hummed.

As Stokely neared the end, Cleve's hums intensified and were accompanied by more and more pronounced gestures. Until finally, he burst into the crescendo of *Try a Little Tenderness*. He even stood and evoked some of Otis' big-man-overwhelmed-with-love gyrations.

They both exploded in laughter. Cleve's antics were perfectly timed. He managed to add humor into what could've been a pity party.

As the laughter subsided, Cleve shifted into full patriarch mode, "Didn't I ever tell you that every shut eye ain't sleep and every goodbye ain't gone?"

Stokely smirked at the memory and said, "Yeah, too many times."

"Shit, you thought I was talking to hear myself speak? Aw nawl, man, I was trying to put you up on some game. You know life lessons and perspective." Cleve looked at his empty smoothie bottle and shook his head.

"See son, I know you well-intended and all. I bet Phoenix knows it too. But this matter ain't one where you can make the outcome happen on sheer will. If you try that, you'd just fuck it up some more." Cleve paused so that the words could sink in.

He resumed, "You are going to need to give her time. In the end, she'd love ya more for it. But she is going to need some time to sort all this shit out. Plus, that's her dad, man - I bet she got a whole lotta questions for him. And see, that's what you're taking personally and that's yo' mistake."

Cleve looked at the smoothie bottle again before adding in a different tone, "If a sweet young thing was serving me this first thing in the morning, I'd drink it too. But ain't no sweet thangs here and this healthy shit is over-rated. It's the memory that so good to you."

They laughed again.

"Sometimes son, the knowing that the love is there is kinda like the life preserver things you see on the boats. You know the circle thangs?" Stokely nodded. "Well, when you on the turbulent seas, knowing you have a life preserver is assuring but your priority is surviving the storm. For Phoenix, meeting dad - that's the storm. Knowing that his wife was yo' ole lady - shit, that's some turbulent seas for yo' ass. But all the good times y'all had, those the life preservers."

Cleve tilted his head toward Stokely with one arched eyebrow as if to say, "Did you get my point?"

"So I'mma say to you like the church folk like to say, 'be yo ass still and know that God is.'"

Stokely nearly spit up the last of his smoothie from laughing.

"Now enough of this sentimental shit unless you want me to start singing Jerry Butler's *Only the Strong Survive*. An idea that spurred another round of laughter.

Then Cleve asked, "When are you gonna pack? You want me to come back tomorrow?"

"Yeah, that'll work. I'll be packed by then."

"If you got your ass to work, with this little shit you got, you'd be packed before lunchtime." Then Cleve looked around and added, "I bet you wish you could get some of that furniture from your house back."

"Actually, I don't. That was then, you know? I'm moving into a new place and I want some new things to fit that place."

"We still talking about your love life, hunh?"

They laughed some more.

ABOUT THE AUTHOR

Sabin Prentis is a husband, father, educator, native Detroiter, and lover of authentic hip-hop. He is the owner of Fielding Books and the author of *Assuming Hurts, Reflections from the Frontline,* and co-author of *Listen Up and Four Floors.*

Creative Team
Tiffany L. Hall ~ Creative Director
La Donna Sims ~ Cover Model
George Mitchell ~ Cover Photography

For more information:
www.sabinprentis.com